Weaver's Lament

ALSO BY EMMA NEWMAN

WEAVER'S LAMENT

INDUSTRIAL MAGIC, BOOK 2

EMMA NEWMAN

A TOM DOHERTY ASSOCIATES BOOK

NEW YORK

WEAVER'S LAMENT

Cover illustration by Cliff Nielsen
Cover design by Christine Foltzer

Edited by Lee Harris

A Tor.com Book
Published by Tom Doherty Associates
175 Fifth Avenue
New York, NY 10010

www.tor.com

Tor® is a registered trademark of
Macmillan Publishing Group, LLC.

ISBN 978-0-7653-9410-1 (ebook)
ISBN 978-0-7653-9411-8 (trade paperback)

First Edition: October 2017

For my Uncle Martin and Auntie Gail,
who have always been there for me

Weaver's Lament

Chapter 1

CHARLOTTE WAS CERTAIN she was going to die. She'd thought the threat of Royal Society Enforcers was the most terrifying thing she'd ever experienced, but that was nothing compared to travelling by train. Now she understood why her grandmother had always crossed herself whenever anyone mentioned the rapidly expanding rail network.

She'd been fine in the first few minutes of the journey, when the train had pulled away from Euston station in a stately fashion, even excited. She'd looked out on transport sheds and then houses, with a sense of adventure blooming in her chest. It wasn't so bad; it was bumpy and noisy as the carriage rattled over the rails, but only a little faster than an omnibus. Quite why her father had looked so concerned when he'd helped her into the carriage, she'd had no idea.

Twenty minutes into the journey, as the city thinned and the countryside opened up, the train had built speed until the greenery at the side of the track was a blur. Surely nothing could go so fast and be safe? No wonder her mother had been so put out by Ben's letter, asking his sister to visit him in Manchester.

"But you'll have to go on the train!" she'd squawked. "It's such a long way! Why can't he come to visit us here?"

"Because he's not allowed," Charlotte had replied, reading the letter from her brother again. It seemed like a simple invitation, but the fact that he'd asked only for her made Charlotte nervous. Surely he missed their parents too? She feared he was getting ill again and struggling to cope. After the success of being accepted into the Royal Society of Esoteric Arts, she could imagine his reluctance to admit any weakness, especially considering the exorbitant amount of money they'd paid her family as compensation. She remembered how proud he'd been, even though it had been *her* magical skill, not his, that had earned him a place in the College of Dynamics and changed their family's fortune.

"But I thought he wasn't allowed to see us," Father had said. "Something must be wrong. I should go with you."

Charlotte knew Ben would be furious if she brought anyone else with her. "No, Papa, I'll go by myself. If there was a problem, he'd have been sent home. We'd know about it. He's probably missing us and can't risk the entire family going to see him."

So much concern over one simple invitation, but it was no surprise. They'd all been worrying about him, and with the six-month mark of his training as a magus coming up, they were all afraid that his previous pattern would resurface; he'd last a few months away from home and then fall deathly ill again.

"I'm not sure it's proper for you to travel alone, Charlotte," Mother had said. "We're a respectable family now. We live in the *West End*. People will talk."

She'd laughed. "Mother, no one will even notice I'm gone! Even George is too busy to see me this week."

Her fiancé's review was on Friday and he was desperate to earn his promotion to registrar. She was certain he'd succeed; the office of Births, Deaths and Marriages could not have a more dedicated clerk. But there was more at stake than his professional pride; he was adamant that they could not marry unless he was earning a decent salary in a secure position. Not even the offer of help from her parents, now very well off thanks to the compensation from the Royal Society for taking Ben, would dissuade him. "It's a matter of principle, darling," he'd said to her. "If I cannot provide a good life for my wife right from the start, I don't deserve to marry."

Charlotte would have been happy to live in a tiny terraced house back over on the other side of the city, where they used to live before the windfall, but she was willing to be patient. Life in the west of the city was surprisingly different. Her mother was so much happier there—she'd been able to give up sewing—and the house was larger, with a better landlord. But with the improvement of their circumstances came a strange set of ideas that Charlotte simply didn't share. Her mother seemed to think that living in the West End meant they had to go prome-nading in the park on Sunday afternoons after church. The colour of their curtains had to be fashionable, they had to have a maid—even though they'd been perfectly fine without one before—and Charlotte had to take care of her reputation. It seemed that taking the train alone would somehow endanger it. Charlotte was certain that her secret career as an illustrator would not fit in with her mother's ideas about how she should conduct her-self, either.

"I will put her on the train at Euston," Father had said, elbow resting on the large mantelpiece, pipe in hand. "Benjamin will meet her at London Road station in Man-chester. The London and North Western railway com-pany has trains that go straight there with no changes. We'll make sure he knows which train she will be on."

"I shall go tomorrow," Charlotte had said. "Then I can be back for Friday, so I can be there for George after his review."

"That's settled, then," Father had said between puffs. It seemed that, for him, their change in fortune had translated to that particular pose and unfortunately smelly habit.

Now she wished her father had come with her, if only just so she would have someone to talk to. She'd brought her sketchbook, handkerchiefs to embroider and some crochet, but was unable to put her hand to any of them. Even though the terror had subsided to a constant tension and a gasp every time the carriage lurched on a corner, it was still too bumpy for her to do anything save look out the window.

Growing accustomed to the speed, Charlotte was getting used to focusing her attention out towards the horizon. It was a beautiful May morning when she left Euston and she was filled with hope as she looked out over the verdant countryside. The hedgerows were flowering, the fresh new leaves on the trees were her favourite shade of pale green and she could see lambs gambolling in the fields. George would be promoted and they would have a spring wedding and it would be perfect. As they sped through the midlands, the sky darkened and the view was obscured by driving rain. At least she was in an enclosed first class carriage. Her grandfather had told her about the old third class carriage he'd travelled in once, open to the elements during a terrible thunderstorm. She shivered at the mere thought of it.

Daydreaming about her wedding and enjoying the view could only keep her fears for Ben at bay for so long. The compartment was relatively small, seating six comfortably, and had its own door. She was lonely, yet always relieved when no one got in to share it with her at a station. She wouldn't know what to do if a man travelling alone got in with her. She hoped another young woman would share the rest of the journey, providing company without any fear of unwelcome attention, but she was still alone hours later when the train pulled into Crewe. A comfort stop of ten minutes was announced, but she didn't want to leave her luggage unattended, so she watched the other passengers instead. She was desperate for a cup of tea and a bun, but she decided to wait until she arrived so she could share that with Ben.

Charlotte was just starting to change her mind when she spotted a familiar flash of blond hair against a black satin collar. She jolted in her seat as she realised the man leaving the compartment next to hers was none other than Magus Hopkins, her secret tutor. The sight of him brought the usual tumult of guilt and excitement. The sense of guilt had started months before, when he'd discovered she'd helped to con the Royal Society into thinking her brother was far more magically gifted than he was. It was a permanent emotion now, reinforced every time they met in secret, even though it was only so he could teach her how to control her own ability without turning wild.

Charlotte watched him stride towards the station café

along with many other passengers. Her heart pounded, as it always did when she saw him. She scowled at the back of his burgundy frock coat, silently cursing the perfection of his silhouette. Like every time she saw him, she was seized by the desire to draw him. Charlotte knew she must never give in to it. Bad enough that she even considered it.

When Hopkins was out of sight, she leaned back so he wouldn't be able to see her through the window of her carriage when he returned to the train. Had he followed her? Surely not! She'd left a note in the usual hiding place, explaining that she couldn't meet him that week, but hadn't said anything about the reason why.

A knock on the window made her jump and she felt her face flush red when she saw a burgundy velvet cuff. She pulled the window down as Magus Hopkins doffed his top hat to her.

"Why, Miss Gunn, it is you!" he said with a cheery smile. "What an extraordinary coincidence!"

"Indeed," she said, trying to hide her delight at seeing his face by frowning most deeply. "What brings you to Crewe?"

"Oh, I'm going to Manchester," he said, patting his hat back into place. "My compartment is next to yours. We've been neighbours all the way from Euston, it would seem."

She folded her arms. "Magus Hopkins, this is too much of a coincidence for me to bear. Why have you followed me?"

His eyebrows shot up behind the brim of his hat. "Followed you? Quite the contrary, Miss Gunn. I've been invited to assist with the design of a new clock tower. The Manchester Reform Club has proposed something quite ambitious."

It sounded plausible enough; his specialisation in the Fine Kinetic arts was the design of efficient timepieces. The Royal Society held the Queen's charter for the maintenance, measurement and accuracy of nationalised timekeeping, necessitated by the rise in popularity of the railways. Now that the country could be crossed in a matter of hours, localised time at individual towns and cities was no longer acceptable. The trains, in turn, were a product of research funded by the College of Thermaturgy, and one of their magi would be at the front of the train now, using Esoteric arts to keep the boiler at exactly the right temperature. Between the three colleges of the Royal Society, England—and indeed, the Empire—were evolving at an astounding rate.

No matter how plausible the reason, Charlotte didn't believe him. But then she considered how she was simply one secret in his life, not the centre of it. She doubted that her comings and goings were of as much interest to him as he was to her. She shouldn't be so vain.

"May I ask what takes you to the North, Miss Gunn?"

She couldn't tell him the real reason. Ben could get into trouble if his supervisors knew he'd written to her. "I'm visiting a relative," she said. "My aunt. Vera. My aunt Vera."

His lip twitched in that maddening, charming way it did whenever he disbelieved her. "Oh, really? I confess, when I spotted you on the way to the café, I was certain you'd be on your way to visit your brother. He's been assigned to a mill in Manchester, has he not?"

That was more than she knew. "I have no idea," she replied truthfully. "Apprentices aren't permitted to disclose their whereabouts to relatives, as you know."

"Shame," Hopkins said, glancing down the platform as other passengers started to return to their compartments. "I've heard some rather alarming rumours about a couple of the cotton mills there. It would have been interesting to know if there was any truth to them."

"What rumours?"

He waved a hand, dismissively. "All hearsay, no doubt. But of course, it's of no relevance to your dear aunt."

The twinkle in his eye infuriated her. Must he always tease her so? "If my brother were—purely hypothetically—serving his apprenticeship in one of those mills, would he be in danger?"

"I would not be content if someone I loved were involved in their operation."

She bit her lip. She knew he was steering her again, as was his wont, but she couldn't let her pride interfere when it came to Ben's safety. "Please, Magus Hopkins, if there's something I should know about my brother's apprenticeship, do tell me. Is this Ledbetter's doing? Is it something to do with that awful cage he was involved in?"

Magus Ledbetter was the one who had recruited her brother into the College of Dynamics, an odious man whose marque was embossed on a cage that killed debtors. With the help of Magus Hopkins, she'd been able to save her father from that fate, but not her brother from Ledbetter's clutches. As much as she feared for Ben's health away from home, she also feared that Ledbetter would corrupt his gentle heart.

Hopkins became serious. "The mills are the province of the College of Dynamics, you understand. They wouldn't appreciate the likes of me knowing about any difficulties they may have, let alone my telling another."

Charlotte slid to the edge of her seat, closing the distance between them. "You said that we would work together, rooting out the likes of Ledbetter and his despicable activities. If there is anything like that cage happening where my brother is apprenticed I insist you tell me."

"He's asked you for help, hasn't he?"

She looked away, torn. "He's asked me to visit," she confessed. "He didn't say anything in the letter, but he asked only for me. I'm very worried."

He nodded, satisfied with the truth. She hated breaking her brother's confidence, but Hopkins had not let her down yet. "There have been several unusual accidents that can't be ascribed to mechanical failure nor to human error. The accounts that have reached me speak of something sinister at play and—"

"Is this gentleman bothering you, Miss?"

Charlotte leaned back as the station guard came into view. "Thank you for your concern, but we are acquainted."

The guard doffed his cap at both her and Hopkins. "Begging your pardon, sir, Miss, but I like to keep an eye out for any young ladies travelling alone."

"Most considerate of you," Hopkins said. "I was simply doing the same."

"The train will be moving on shortly," the guard said. "May I suggest you return to your compartment, sir?"

Hopkins doffed his hat to Charlotte again. "I wish you a very pleasant stay in Manchester, Miss Gunn." He looked as if he were about to go, but reconsidered. "And *mark* my words, Miss Gunn. You are likely to see things in Manchester that will upset you, and possibly test even a saint's temper. Best to keep your mind on higher things."

He was warning her to be mindful of his teachings and remember her own marque. As an untrained latent magus, the risk of turning wild was omnipresent for her. In the months that had passed since Ben's test, she knew she was getting more powerful, and Hopkins had confirmed as much. He had taught her the technique her brother would also have learned to manage his ability. Like all the magi, she'd developed her own personal symbol, what the Royal Society referred to as a "marque." It was meaningful only to her, and focusing upon it helped to rein in her latent ability. It would also, in time, mean that she'd be able to influence objects at a distance, even out of her sight.

She wanted to ask Hopkins to come into the compartment with her so they could continue the conversation, but she didn't dare do something so scandalous in front of the guard. Besides, Ben was meeting her at the station, and if he met her straight of the train, he'd recognise Hopkins. They'd met when Ben was tested. All she could do was give a faint smile and say, "Thank you, Magus Hopkins. I will bear that in mind."

The guard saw Hopkins to his compartment and gave her a kindly smile as he walked off down the platform. Charlotte wished she'd gotten that cup of tea after all. She needed one now more than ever.

Chapter 2

THE CROWDED PLATFORM at London Road station was both a blessing and a curse. It reduced any chance that Ben might have had to spot Hopkins, but it also made it very difficult for her to be seen, too.

It was easy to pick Ben out in the crowd, as he stood at least a foot taller than many of the men there. But no matter how much she waved at him, he simply didn't see her. She dragged her bag from her compartment and stood on it, taking off her bonnet to flap it at him. At last, he waved at her and made his way over, cutting through the crowd like a tea clipper.

He picked her up and span her around. "Charlie Bean!" he cheered. "Oh, I am so very glad to see you!"

"Put me down, silly!" Charlotte laughed, worried that far too much of her petticoat lace was in plain sight. She beamed up at him when he put her down.

He looked so well! Better than she'd ever seen him, in fact. His gaunt cheeks had filled out and even taken on a rosy hue. His dark brown hair was shining, his sideburns and moustache neatly clipped, his back straight. The coat hanger quality of his shoulders had gone and he filled out his shirt and frock coat with a broad chest. His arms had felt strong when he'd picked her up. He was the very picture of health.

"How was the journey?"

"Terrifying," she said, and he chuckled. "It improved once I got used to it. Could you wave that porter over?"

"No need," he said, picking up her bag as if it contained tissue paper. "There are splendid tearooms down the road. Are you thirsty?"

"Parched," she said, tucking her hand into the crook of his elbow. "It's so lovely to see you again!"

Charlotte clung to him as he led her through the crowd, Hopkins nowhere to be seen in the throng of passengers. They passed happy reunions and tearful farewells, until at last they made it out onto the street.

Ben disentangled himself from her. "I'm afraid we shouldn't be seen to be close, out on the street," he said. "Sorry, Charlie, I quite forgot myself there. I shouldn't have embraced you like that. Not in public."

She looked around them, but no one seemed to be paying any attention. "I understand," she said.

Out on the street, the red-bricked buildings made her feel a world away from the fine Georgian stone and grey bricks of London. The street was pulsing with people and the thoroughfare was clogged with horse-drawn carriages and omnibuses. The skyline was dominated by mills several storeys high, mixed with rows of workers' cottages and slums. The smell was most unpleasant, and Charlotte couldn't help but think of miasma. Only two years before, thousands had died here from cholera.

Despite the overcrowding and filth of the city, she was happy to be there. It was such a relief to see Ben well. The ominous comments Hopkins had made about the mills seemed irrelevant now. Ben seemed full of confidence and people moved out of their way as he approached. He wore the red-and-black-striped cravat of a Dynamics apprentice, and those who noticed it stared at him as they passed with looks of envy, fear, and respect. How different it was from the last time they'd walked down a street together and she'd had to practically carry him home. This time she was hurrying to keep up.

She was glad when he guided her towards the doors of the Heywood Tea Rooms. "You must try an Eccles cake," he said as he held the door open for her. "They are quite extraordinary."

It was a very large establishment, filled with tables covered in crisp white linen waited on by pretty women in smart uniforms. Along the back wall, there were private booths. Charlotte suspected they were the reason he'd brought her here. When Ben asked one of the waitresses to seat them in the one in the far corner, she was certain of it.

He ordered tea for two and Eccles cakes for both of them.

"Mother and Father send their love," she said, watching him cast an eye over the room and the rest of the patrons.

Relaxing, Ben gave her his full attention. "Did they make a fuss about you coming to visit?"

"Of course. They're both well. George, too—he has his review for promotion on Friday. We're hoping for a spring wedding. And there's going to be another collection by the author of *Love, Death and Other Magicks* and I've been commissioned to illustrate it. That's all my news, now you tell me everything!"

The waitress arrived with their order and Ben waited until she'd left again. He sighed at the way Charlotte prodded the Eccles cake. "It's got lots of currants inside. You'll like it."

"When you said 'cake' I was expecting a sponge, not something covered in flaked pastry." She stirred the teapot. "When I got your letter I was worried you'd fallen ill again."

"I've never felt better."

The first pour from the pot was enough to tell her it hadn't brewed long enough. She nibbled at the edge of the pastry and took a larger bite, weathering his "I told you so" expression with as much grace as she could muster. She looked at him expectantly, deciding not to say another word until he started talking.

Instead, he stirred the teapot, too, and then poured for both of them. She took another bite and looked at the rest of the tearooms. Perhaps everything was actually just fine, and she'd got herself into a stew over nothing.

"Charlie, I need your help."

Perhaps not. She looked at him, at his healthy glow, and saw genuine worry in his eyes. "Tell me what's wrong."

"It's all been going so well," he said. "I was so nervous when I left home, I didn't eat for the first couple of days. But then I made a friend, and I settled in and . . . it's difficult, dear heart; we're not really supposed to tell an outsider about anything we do."

Outsider? The word stung. She pushed the feeling down as best she could. "I understand. Has something gone wrong? Is it your friend?"

"No, no, nothing like that. It was very difficult at the start, I won't lie. I struggled terribly but then I had a real breakthrough, and since then I've been doing so well, Charlie. Ledbetter says I'm one of the most promising students he's had for years. Oh, don't look like that! Surely you're not still harbouring that grudge against him!"

"He is not a good man," she said firmly.

"Is this some nonsense about him taking me away from you?"

"Oh, what rot! I'm not a child, Ben!"

"Then tell me what you have against him!"

She picked up her teacup, knowing she could never tell him about that awful debtor's cage. It would put him in an impossible position, and she couldn't risk his success. Now that the Royal Society had recruited him, he could never leave. She wasn't prepared to make his life there a misery, and it would be, if he knew what his mentor was really like. "It's just a feeling I have," she finally said, hating the insipid statement. "You've been doing well," she said, trying to bring him back on topic, if only to take the look of exasperation from his face. "So why did you send for me? Are you lonely? Homesick?"

He shook his head, clearly struggling to confess his troubles. He was such a loyal soul. It didn't stop her from wanting to shake him until he spat it all out, though. She took out her frustration on the cake instead.

"I've been apprenticed to a cotton mill," he finally said, "and it's been going very well. Very well indeed."

"Darling"—she reached across to hold his hand—"you don't have to keep saying that."

He sighed. "I don't want you to think I can't cope. I can, I swear it. In fact, I've never been happier."

"Oh, for heaven's sake, Ben! Just tell me!"

He pulled his hand back and leaned forwards to whisper over the teapot. "There have been a few . . . incidents at the mill. Not on my shifts, I hasten to add. Looms have been destroyed and none of the witnesses are willing to tell us who did it. They're all covering something up."

"Have you spoken to Ledbetter about it?"

"I tried. He just kept brushing me off. I'm only an apprentice, Charlie. No one listens to me and no one explains anything to me except exactly what I need to know."

"It sounds like it's all out of your hands."

"If only it were that simple. I'm being put up to the next level of apprenticeship, which means I won't just be working the line shaft, I'll be supervising the running of the mill as a whole. Ledbetter has a system, you see, to push the best apprentices to the top faster. I've been chosen as one of the final two. Myself and another apprentice, Paxton, are going to be competing against each other. I cannot risk one of these incidents happening when I'm responsible for the mill."

"Is there no one you can confide in? Is that why you asked me to come?"

He poured more tea. "No, that's not it. Charlie, it's more complicated than that. We believe the looms are being destroyed by saboteurs."

"Like the Luddites? Darling, all of that stopped well before we were born!"

"Not Luddites, trade unionists. And more than that, *socialists*." He looked around the tearoom again, lowering his voice further. "There are secret organisations springing up all over the country, determined to wreak havoc. They hate the Royal Society and want to destroy us. They argue that we have too much power and that parliament values the needs of the Royal Society above those of the common man. It's dangerous, Charlie. Sedition, that's what it is. And I'm convinced they have a secret group working at the mill. They have a great number of sympathisers among the workforce, and that's why none of them will out the culprits."

Want to destroy us . . . His words widened the gap between them. Sedition? Socialists? It sounded more like sensationalism to her. Was the pressure getting to him? "Darling, is there something you want me to do? I can't see how I can help."

He lifted the pot to pour tea before realising he'd only just done that. She steeled herself. What was he finding so difficult to say?

"Charlie, I need you to come and work at the mill."

"I beg your pardon?"

"I need you to pretend you're not my sister and just be one of them. One of the workers. I need someone on the inside, and you're so kind and people open up to you so easily."

"Good lord! You want me to be a spy?"

He twitched and looked around the room yet again. No one was sitting close enough to them to listen in. "Keep your voice down! I wouldn't ask if it weren't absolutely imperative. Please, Charlie. None of them will talk to me because I'm a magus. Ledbetter has said that if neither Paxton nor I root out the saboteurs, he'll consider us to be socialist sympathisers. Paxton is a snake, and I am certain he's already trying to pin it all on me. I caught him going through the drawers in my room the other day. He didn't take anything but it's clear he aims to win this round and be fully qualified, no matter the cost." He reached across the table and took her hands. She was shocked to feel them shaking. "Charlie . . . if Paxton pins the socialist problem on me, Ledbetter will have me prosecuted for aiding and abetting sedition."

"But that's utterly ridiculous! Why waste a good apprentice on such an exercise when it isn't your fault?"

"Because he has to make an example. And he has to get to the bottom of it all. Threatening us with transportation is an excellent motivator. In Ledbetter's opinion, anyway."

Charlotte felt sick. "Transportation? To Australia?"

He nodded, just as pale-faced as she was. "I doubt I

would survive the voyage. You know how sickly I used to be. Packed into a boat with criminals rife with disease, I'd be done for."

"Shush," she said, squeezing his hands. "It doesn't bear thinking about." Her misgivings about being a spy faded into insignificance, now that she understood the threat to him.

"You're the only person I can trust completely to tell me who is responsible for the sabotage. I have to root them out, Charlie, before Paxton finds a way to pin it all on me. If I win this round, Ledbetter will pass me for full qualification. Paxton won't be able to touch me. And when I'm fully qualified, I'll be able to apply for funding to build my own mill, with his support. Then I can earn enough money to support you and Mother and Father."

"I don't need you to support me. I'll have George."

Ben leaned back. "You haven't told him, then. About your gift."

She dabbed at her lips with her napkin. "I am not going to discuss that with you. I have everything under control. I'll help, darling, of course I will. But I have heard some horrible stories about mills . . ."

"The London rags exaggerate things terribly," he said. "And it won't be for more than a couple of days. You're such a good judge of character, you'll spot who the ringleader is quickly, I'm sure you will."

"So now I'm a good judge of character? Even th
don't believe me about Ledbetter?" There was a lo
long enough for her to regret her tone. "I'm sorry," she said.
"This is all a bit of a shock. I thought I was going to have
nurse you back to health, not go and work in a mill."

"I know this is horribly selfish of me," Ben said. "But
I'm desperate, Charlie. Help me to find the ringleader,
and I'll make sure you'll never want for anything ever
again."

She tutted at him. "I won't help you for financial gain,
you fool. I'll do it because I love you."

His relief brightened his whole face. She could see
how much it weighed upon him. "Thank you, dear heart,
thank you. I promise it won't be for more than a couple
of days. I'll take care of all the arrangements. Let's have
supper somewhere first, though, shall we?"

Charlotte nodded, feeling bad that she'd made him
think she'd only agreed out of love for him. Hopkins said
something strange was happening at the mills, and he'd
made it sound like something esoteric, rather than political. She was determined to find something that could
be used against Ledbetter, something she could take to
Hopkins so they could build a case. The hope that it
would impress her handsome tutor had nothing to do
with it whatsoever.

Chapter 3

CHARLOTTE STOOD AT THE entrance to a large cobbled yard, trying to muster the courage to go in. LEDBETTER MILLS was written in large iron letters, filling the arch above the railings, with PRINCE STREET written in smaller ones below. There was the mill, huge and imposing, four storeys high with dozens of small windows and then two red-brick buildings on either side of it. One was the men's lodging house; the other was for the women.

The yard was empty and it was almost eight o'clock in the evening. She was tired from the journey and feeling horribly out of sorts. She was wearing an old cotton dress that Ben had given her, with a rather threadbare underdress that had seen better days. She'd changed in an empty worker's cottage nearby which Ben had taken her to after they'd dined together. When she first saw the clothes, she'd refused to wear them; with the ground-in dirt around the hem and cuffs and stains in the armpits of the underdress, she'd thought they were unwashed. They'd argued, Ben explaining that they were simply stained, rather than dirty, and needed to look used so she wouldn't stick out like a sore thumb. She couldn't deny that her hooped crinoline would be the most ridiculous thing to turn up in. She'd given in after reminding herself not to be unreasonable when her brother's freedom—and possibly his life—were at stake.

She had a bundle of bed linens under her arm, a spare underdress, clean smalls, and her hairbrush. Hidden in the centre of the bundle were her sketchbook and a solitary pencil. Ben had told her she shouldn't take it with her, but she couldn't bear the thought of having nothing to give her mind comfort. Besides, it was compact and brand new, bought specially for travel. There was nothing in its pages that could incriminate her. Her crinoline, pretty dresses, crochet and embroidery were left with Ben, who promised to keep it all safe whilst she was working undercover. He'd obviously planned ahead, and must have been confident that she'd say yes. They'd arranged to meet at the same cottage the next evening.

Shaking with nerves, Charlotte took a hesitant step into the courtyard. Ben said that the lodging house was expecting her—or rather, expecting a Charlotte Baker—and that she should go straight there. It hadn't escaped her notice that he'd picked the surname she illustrated under. "Charles Baker" was a successful illustrator of a best-selling poetry collection. If anyone knew that

Charles was actually a woman about to go to work in a cotton mill, there would probably be angry letters sent to the *Times*. Even the thought of portly gentry, red in the face with outrage, didn't make her giggle like it usually did. She was genuinely afraid.

There were stories of rampant disease, thievery and even accidents that caused mutilation and death, all with the mills at the centre of them. Some had speculated that the miasma behind the '48 cholera outbreak had originated in these huge buildings. George had told her that was nonsense. His friend, Dr Snow, had all but convinced him it had something to do with water, rather than the air. It made no sense to Charlotte, not when the learned men of the day all agreed that where there was a foul stench, disease was sure to follow.

It didn't smell particularly sanitary where she stood now. She bit her lip and thought of Ben. Surely if it really were as bad as the papers said, he wouldn't dream of asking her to do this? He had said the stories were exaggerated. Yes, that must be true. He loved her and wouldn't risk any harm coming to her. Besides, she'd seen engravings and paintings of mill workers at galleries in London. Everyone looked strong and the picture of health in those.

Rallying herself, she started off for the lodging house as a loud bell rang inside the mill. When she was halfway across the yard, the mill's doors opened and workers spilled out of the building like water from a sluice gate. She stopped and stared at them as they shuffled to their respective lodging houses.

They were dirty and looked pale; many of them looked sickly. Shoulders slumped, backs curved unnaturally and children limped with deformed knees. They all looked exhausted, pulling neckerchiefs free to mop at their faces. There was a lot of coughing. Conversation was a low hum, rather than the usual roar of any crowd she'd ever seen.

No magi emerged with them, and she remembered Ben talking about how they were kept separate. On the way to the mill, she'd expressed a concern about Ledbetter recognising her, but Ben had assured her that the magus was overseeing the construction of a new mill up in Bury and rarely came to this one. Looking at the workers, Charlotte could understand why Ledbetter stayed away. Who would want to be reminded of these poor souls?

"Are you lost, love?"

A woman, whose age was hard to pin down to anything besides older than Charlotte, had peeled off from the flow of people and come over to her. There were dark circles under her eyes and she looked just as shattered as the rest, but there was something kind about her smile that Charlotte warmed to immediately. "I've come to work here."

"'Ave ye now?" The woman's voice had the same sort of soft Lancashire accent as the Thermaturgy magus who'd tested Ben. "You're not from round 'ere, are yer?"

Charlotte shook her head. "I come from London."

The woman looked her up and down, frowning. "First time ye've needed to work?"

"In a mill, yes." Charlotte didn't dare say she already worked as an illustrator and had sometimes helped Mother with her sewing work. Compared to what this woman did to earn a living, it seemed ridiculous to even call it work.

"'Ard times can fall on us all." The woman sighed. "I'm Marjory, but everyone 'ere calls me Mags. I reckon you'll be in the same dorm as me—there's a bed free there now. You'll be next to Dotty. She's a kind girl and she's your age. You'll be fine. C'mon."

"Thank you," Charlotte said, falling into step with her. "I'm Charlotte. But everyone calls me Charlie."

"Pleased to meet you, Charlie. Keep yer 'ead down, do as yer told and don't complain. You'll be 'right."

Charlotte saw a broad-chested, well-dressed man come round the side of the mill and go over to a shorter man watching the workers leave. He was wearing the same cravat as her brother and had collar-length light brown hair. Mags noted her interest in him. "That's Apprentice Paxton," she whispered. "Keep out of his way, love. He likes nothing more than to lord it over us all, and if he don't like the look of yer, yer out. We don't 'ave nothin' to do with them magi, and that's the way it should be."

So that was the man determined to see her brother transported. Charlotte tore her eyes away from him, lest he notice her. Would he see a family resemblance between her and Ben? The thought made her turn away completely.

Mags steered her through the process of being confirmed as a new employee, taking her to the "right people to 'ave the right things written in the right books," as she put it. Her first shift started at five the following morning. It had been a while since she'd been up that early. Since moving house, Charlotte hadn't had to get up to light the stove. She had a new appreciation for the maid her mother had hired.

"What time does my shift finish?" She hoped to go and find where Hopkins was staying, just so she knew where to find him if she dug up something particularly damning.

Mags gave her a strange look. "Eight o'clock. You saw us all comin' out, didn't yer?"

"I thought that would be the second shift."

Mags cackled. "Oh, you poor lamb. You're in for a shock. Working in t'mill is tougher than any fancy-pants

London jobs, I can tell you that now. Let's find Dotty, she can take you round. I'm shattered."

Mags took her up two flights of a dingy stairwell and down a long corridor. Most of the doors off it were open and Charlotte could see rows of beds inside, about twenty to a room. There was no privacy to speak of. She followed Mags to a room at the end, where Mags waved a hand at the bed nearest to the window. It looked onto the red-bricked wall of the mill next door, practically in arm's reach. "That's yours, Charlie. Dotty, come and say 'ello to the new girl."

There were several women there, most of them younger than her, lying fully clothed on top of the beds. The chatter had stopped and everyone stared at Charlotte. Mags was the eldest, and from the way Dotty leaped up from her bed, it seemed authority came with age.

"'Ello," Dotty said with a shy smile as Charlotte went to her bed.

"Hello," Charlotte replied. "Don't you want this bed? It's by the window." Even though there was no view, there was fresh air to be had.

Several of the other women sniggered. "Now you lot," Mags said sternly. "Charlie's new and won't 'ave any of you lording over her just cos she don't know 'er arse from 'er elbow. Charlie, love, no one wants that bed cos it's cold as buggery by the window when winter comes. It's all yours."

The narrow metal-framed bed was covered with a scratchy grey wool blanket. When Charlotte pulled that back, she saw that old, dirty sheets were still on it. Thank goodness Ben had given her clean bed linen. She opened the window and started to strip the bed as Dotty watched.

"Where you from then?"

"London. I've never worked at a mill before. Have you been here long?"

"Since I were ten. Me family stuck it out on the farm for as long as they could, but it were 'opeless. When my brother died, we upped sticks and started again."

"I'm so sorry. About your brother."

Dotty shrugged. "He were little and the 'arvest failed that year. It were 'orrible. Only me left now. What about you?"

Charlotte almost said she had a brother, but it seemed insensitive, and besides, she had to be careful. She needed a cover story, something to make it sound plausible for her to have ended up here. "My mother and father died a couple of years ago. I was married, but my husband . . ." she hesitated. Lying was something she did far too much of as it was, hiding her magical abilities and her art, but this felt even more sordid.

"Drink or gamblin'?"

She couldn't decide. "Both," she said, fixing an image of the archetypical villain from some penny dreadful story. "He gambled away all our money and drowned in the Thames."

Dotty's brown eyes were huge with horror, tinged with a hint of grim fascination. "So what brought you up 'ere, then?"

Charlotte was briefly distracted by the stains on the sheets and the stench of urine. She had to sleep on this? "Oh, well, I had relatives nearby, but they died, too. I didn't have anywhere else to go. What should I do with these sheets?"

"There's a washing room downstairs. Want me to show you round? It's nearly time for supper anyway."

Charlotte nodded and started off for the door, but Mags rested a hand on her shoulder. "Take yer bundle, love," she whispered. "There's some light fingers 'ere."

Blushing, Charlotte retrieved her belongings. Dotty gathered up the dirty sheets, rolling them up without even wrinkling her nose.

"This is one of the better mills," Dotty said as Charlotte retraced her steps back to the stairwell. "They take twelve shillings a week from yer pay but you get three meals and yer bedclothes washed for you. You can use the washing room on Sundays if you wish, but you can

41

pay a shilling to add something to the group wash and it'll be cleaned and dried with the sheets. Boil wash and all." She leaned back to whisper, "I do my own smalls, though. Can't stand the thought of anyone else goin' near 'em."

Charlotte nodded, hoping she would be gone before she had to wash anything. She was shown the washroom and the courtyard at the back, with its dozens of washing lines. The old sheets were dumped in a big basket with others and soon forgotten about.

"Supper's at 'alf eight," Dotty said. "And the food's really good. You get a bread roll with every meal! Not like them other mills where they don't put on any food at all. You get an egg in the morning with a rasher of bacon on Sundays, meat and potatoes for lunch and soup for supper. You're dead lucky they had an openin' for you. I've heard that Cartwright's mills 'ave started puttin' food on for the workers, but it's all the old scraps that no one else wants to buy from the 'olesalers. And there's maggots in the meat! I'll show you where the privy is and the water pump so we can wash up for supper."

The privy was a stinking shack at the far end of the yard. Charlotte resolved that she would just have to hold everything in. Her face must have said as much.

"We all use the pot. There'll be one under yer bed. If you pay a penny a week to the cook's son, he'll collect yours up with ours every morning and every evening. Don't look like that! It could be so much worse! Them's that work at Cartwright's end up in the slums. They 'ave to put bricks down to stand on so you can get across the street without treading in shit. People just chuck it out onto the street there."

Dotty took her to the hand pump at the back of the building, and they drew water for each other to wash their hands and faces. Charlotte noticed how hard it seemed for Dotty to work the handle. "I'm no use to man nor beast by the end of shift," she said with grim cheer. "I'll be 'right after supper. We tell stories and have a sing-song sometimes, in the dorm, y'know. They're not a bad bunch, really. In the dorm I was in before, one of the women took a disliking to me and 'it me all the time."

Charlotte was glad she had her bundle to cling to as they queued at the hatch to the kitchen. The dining room was filled with long tables and benches and in the last of the evening light, it didn't seem too bad. She'd always known she'd been lucky to have the life she did. Her parents had always made it clear that she and Ben had a much easier childhood than they had had. And her grandparents had all been farmers, so she knew how hard a life it was. But it was only now, as she stood in borrowed clothes, that Charlotte really, truly appreciated how lucky she was.

She listened to the chatter around them, but there was no mention of any incidents. Dotty told her about the foreman and how horrible he was. She talked about the looms she managed and how to work them, but for every word Charlotte recognised, there were three she had never heard before.

Supper was watery soup with cabbage and anaemic chunks of what might have been mutton. Charlotte hoped it was mutton. It smelt of dishwater. Dotty tucked in with relish, but Charlotte was unable to muster the will to even try it. Thank goodness Ben had taken her out to eat earlier; her belly was still full from the steak and kidney pie she'd enjoyed with him.

"Do y'not want that?" Dotty asked as she finished her bread roll.

"I think I'm a bit nervous," Charlotte said truthfully. "I haven't got any appetite. You have it."

She pushed it across the table and Dotty stared at her. "Really?" At Charlotte's nod she spooned the soup into her mouth like she hadn't eaten for days. The way her eyes sparkled with happiness made Charlotte want to cry.

"I'm going to go and make my bed," she said to Dotty, unwilling to sit there and watch her eat for a moment longer.

"I won't be long," Dotty said through a mouthful of soggy bread. "I'll see y'up there."

Charlotte went the wrong way to start with, but then realised there was more than one stairwell and eventually found the correct corridor. The gas lamps had been lit, but they were so widely spaced she had to go through pools of darkness to get to the dorm. With relief, Charlotte didn't hear any conversation coming from the room as she approached. She wanted a few minutes alone to gather her wits, steady herself and find somewhere to hide her sketchbook.

But there was someone on her bed when she arrived at the doorway; a woman with her back to the door, lying on her side. For a moment, Charlotte thought she'd made another mistake, but then she saw the open window and recognised the fresh bed linen. "Excuse me," she said, but the woman didn't stir. "Excuse me," Charlotte repeated, stepping inside the room. "I'm afraid that's my bed." The woman continued to ignore her. She was probably asleep. Charlotte approached the bed, feeling bad for disturbing her. "I'm so sorry, but that's my bed," she repeated.

"Who are yer talkin' to?"

Dotty was standing at the entrance to the door, frowning at her.

Charlotte pointed at the bed. "That lady—" But when she looked back, the bed was empty. She shivered. "I thought someone was on my bed."

"Want an 'and tuckin' in your sheets?" Dotty asked.

"Thank you," she mumbled. It was probably just a shadow playing tricks with her eyes. Charlotte had the feeling she wasn't going to sleep well that night.

Chapter 4

WHEN THE BELL RANG to rouse the workers from their rest, Charlotte groaned. She'd lain awake most of the night, listening to the snoring and coughing and creaking beds of the other women around her. When she'd heard the chimes of the clock tower bells at midnight, she wondered where Hopkins was and what he would have to say about this. None of the imagined comments were very nice.

She shuffled about with the others, dressing and readying themselves for the day, all too tired to care about who saw or heard what. It was still dark outside. In the dining hall the bread rolls and boiled eggs were there to collect, peel and eat. Charlotte almost asked where the salt was and thought against it. She didn't want to draw any attention to herself.

More than anything, though, even more than sleep, she wanted the opportunity to sketch what she saw. She wanted to study the lines on these women's faces and capture the way their bodies had been shaped by their labour. As she picked a rogue fragment of eggshell from her teeth, Charlotte daydreamed about teaming up with

a London journalist to put together an exposé of life behind the mill walls, or perhaps creating an oil painting
that actually showed the truth, rather than the sanitised,
romantic depictions of mill ladies she had seen. She remembered the crowd gathered around one picture set in
an absurdly clean street, all the women with Rubenesque
bodies and flawless white skin, hair attractively tousled
instead of hanging limp and greasy. Now she knew why
that painting had been so popular. That portrayal reas-
sured people who didn't like to think about what life was
really like for those less fortunate. No one wanted to see
what the cotton mill workers really looked like, because
then they'd have to think about *why* they looked this way.

Another bell rang just as she was finishing her roll.
"Come on, then!" Dotty said, heaving her up. "Time to
get goin'!"

They joined the press of people trudging into the mill.
Charlotte drew looks and comments from a variety of
people, which she'd expected as the new girl, but that
didn't make it any easier. If George saw where she was
now, he'd have a heart attack.

The foreman, a red-cheeked man with an impressive
set of jowls and a receding hair line, was just outside the
doors. Now that she was standing next to him, instead
of looking at him from across a courtyard, Charlotte realised she was slightly taller than him. He looked her up

and down, looking doubtful. "'Ave you ever worked a Lancashire loom before, lass?" When she shook her head he puffed out his cheeks. "What about cardin'?" At her blank expression, he added, "Gettin' the wool ready to be spun." He tutted when she shook her head. "Well, you're too big to clean underneath . . ."

"I can teach 'er the looms," Dotty said. "I don't mind."

"I don't want you distracted."

"I won't be. You know 'ow quick I am."

The foreman scratched his chin. "I won't make any allowances for yer." When Dotty nodded, he looked at Charlotte. "You can watch an' learn. Y'won't get paid until you're manning the looms yerself, so pay attention. A'right?"

Charlotte nodded and they were ushered inside.

"Thank you," Charlotte whispered to Dotty. "That was very kind."

"We all 'ave to start somewhere," Dotty whispered back.

The room spanned the entirety of the ground floor, save the space given to the stairwell that ran to the upper floors, and there were dozens and dozens of looms in perfectly straight rows. Charlotte had never seen anything so daunting. There were huge shafts of metal running along the ceiling above each row of looms, with wide belts of leather running from the shaft to each loom. Each one was the size of the old kitchen table, with hundreds of threads stretched over two wooden frames. There were cogs and levers and none of it made any sense to her.

The air was stuffy, even though the sun was only just coming up, and none of the windows were open. The foreman was making sure everyone was in position, and there was a strange tension in the air. Everything felt far too still.

"I look after these ones," Dotty said in a whisper as she pointed to four in front of her and four behind her. "You'll 'ave to watch closely, as I 'ave to move quick when I'm workin' and I won't be able to talk to you."

"Why not?" Charlotte whispered back.

"I 'ave to keep it clean, check for thread breakages and replace the empty bobbin. The wooden thing the bobbin goes into is called the shuttle. These new looms stop when the thread runs out, but I 'ave to get it going again as quick as possible, otherwise I get a strappin'."

"A what?"

She didn't seem to hear that question, either. "The little uns'll be crawling around, getting the fluff and piecin' for me if it's one of the lower warp yarns that's broke. So watch where y'step, 'right?"

Another bell was rung. Everyone seemed to hold their breath. Then the noise began. The shafts running along the ceiling started revolving, which in turn drove the belts that set the looms off. The clattering din hurt Charlotte's ears, and she covered them in surprise, making Dotty laugh and roll her eyes.

Charlotte was amazed at the speed of the looms. She soon worked out that the two frames held the warp yarns apart so the shuttle could be passed between them before being switched over for the shuttle to pass back, forming the weave of the cloth. The shuttle went so fast she couldn't see it, and if Dotty hadn't pointed it out before, she never would have spotted it.

The temperature in the room began to climb, and soon Charlotte could feel sweat running down her back. It wasn't just the heat, but also the humidity, and it felt as if it were getting harder to breathe. The air seemed to thicken, motes of dust and tiny fibres from the cotton sparkling in the first shafts of sunlight hitting the room. As the sun climbed, Charlotte simply couldn't understand why no one was opening the windows. Thinking they were too tied to their duties at the looms, she headed towards the nearest one, only for Dotty to grab her arm and shake her head, mouthing a definite "no" to her.

Small girls and boys were crawling beneath the machines, gathering up clumps of cotton fluff and stuffing them into cloth satchels. She watched one boy scoot over to a machine that had been stopped. Charlotte crouched to see his little fingers deftly tying a broken strand of yarn. The machine was soon started again, the operator not even checking if the child's fingers were clear. It was only then that she noticed one of them missing the top half of an index finger.

Charlotte bit her lip. Had it been lost in an accident here? And now that she was looking, she could see other people with maimed hands. One man's right arm hung limp at his side, yet he was still managing eight looms with the help of a small girl who did the thread tying for him.

Dotty tapped her shoulder and pointed at one of her looms which had stopped working. She pulled out the shuttle and dropped a new one into place, tied something and set the loom off again in a matter of seconds. Going back to the shuttle she'd just removed, she lifted up the empty bobbin and pulled it off a spike of metal in the centre, then dropped it in a bucket by the side of the loom. She pulled a new bobbin thick with spun thread from a metal bucket resting nearby, dropped it over the spike of metal and flipped that back into place, then put the end of the shuttle to her mouth. When she moved it away, Charlotte could see the end of the thread coming out of a hole at the shuttle's tip. It was put into the place the replacement bobbin had been, ready to be swapped in again. In moments, the next machine along needed to have its bobbin replaced and Charlotte trailed after Dotty, trying to work out where the new thread was tied.

She worked so fast that each loom was still for only

about fifteen seconds. And she didn't rest between the bobbin changes. Dotty was constantly vigilant, checking the cloth being produced, wiping the edges of the machine down, constantly checking and rechecking the state of the threads.

And all the while, the temperature rose. Charlotte's head was pounding. Her feet hurt. The noise was unbearable. No one could talk to each other but she did notice a couple of people mouthing words across looms and seeming to understand each other. She could see people coughing, even though she couldn't hear them, and by midmorning she was coughing, too, feeling a persistent tickle at the back of her throat that she simply couldn't shift.

Surely there had to be a break soon? It felt like days since the shift had begun. The sun's steady rise, something that usually lifted her heart, filled her with dread as the factory's temperature became unbearable. She had to get outside and breathe in some fresh air! She had to tell Ben that this was never going to work!

The bell was rung and the shafts stopped turning, bringing the drive belts to rest and the looms to a stop. Charlotte's ears were ringing and she could still hear the clattering of the looms even though they'd stopped. Dotty said something to her and she couldn't hear her. Panicking, she pushed her way through the press of workers, fearing she was about to collapse as she was squeezed in the throng, and then she was staggering into the cobbled yard, sucking in great lungfuls of air.

Gradually, Charlotte became aware of people laughing at her, but instead of being embarrassed, she could only be grateful she could actually hear their jeers. Dotty hurried over and rubbed her back as Charlotte braced her hands on her knees, coughing.

"I knew you'd find it 'ard," Dottie said. "Bugger off, you lot!" she shouted at some of the kids who were mocking Charlotte's distress. "It'll get easier. I promise. Come on, we 'ave to get our lunch. We've only got twenty minutes."

"I thought it was half an hour!" Charlotte said, but Dottie shook her head.

"We 'ave to clean the machines before they start up again. Only quick like. C'mon."

The food was being served at the long tables this time—there was no time for queuing after all—and soon there was a plate of some fatty beef chunks and a helping of boiled potatoes in front of her. A pitcher of water was passed down the table to refill glasses and Charlotte was so thirsty she drank it, despite the fact it was cloudy. She could imagine George's rage if he saw her do that, given his friend's beliefs.

Her feet throbbed and her ears were still ringing. She'd been in that mill for only seven hours and hadn't even been working, just learning the job, but she was exhausted. Her heart pounded too fast at the thought of going back into that oven. She simply couldn't bear the thought of it. She picked at the meat, unable to stomach it, had a couple of the potato chunks and then pushed the plate over to Dotty. "Here," she said. "You have this. Thank you for looking after me."

Dotty looked up from her own plate, mouth full. "What y'doin'?"

Charlotte put her bread roll next to the crumbs left on Dotty's plate. "No one should live like this," she muttered and got up.

"Where y'goin'?" Dotty called, but Charlotte kept walking, unable to say that she was going to find her brother.

She left the dining hall, ignoring the foreman who watched her go by with a frown on his face, and went back to the mill. She had to find where the magi worked.

She'd arranged to meet Ben at sunset back at the worker's cottage where she'd changed her clothes the day before. She couldn't wait until then.

Ben would be involved in making the line shafts turn; he'd said as much and from what she'd seen in there, it was the only thing a magus of the Dynamics college could do. The looms contained too many parts in concert for anyone other than a Fine Kinetics magus to control, though a Dynamics magus could turn the drive belt. It was far more efficient for them to turn the main line shafts, however, driving hundreds of looms at once.

She'd noticed how the ends of the shafts went through square gaps in the far wall to allow them to turn unimpeded, so whatever the magi did to turn them had to be on the other side of it. Having endured the morning in that place, she now knew why they were kept separate. She reasoned that they must have their own way in round the back of the mill.

There was indeed another entrance, with doors that had ornate brass handles and a dressed stone portico framing them. Leading up to the doors was a neat flagstoned path running from the boundary of the mill site, an entirely separate set of iron gates at the end of it. They were, unsurprisingly, more ornate than the gates she'd passed through the night before.

The ground floor windows on this side of the mill were larger, but the lower sills were too high for her to be able to look inside. She tried the doors but they were locked. She didn't even know if Ben was in there. She couldn't shout for him; she didn't want to draw attention to herself or, more important, to him. He'd get into trouble if people discovered the relationship between them.

Leaning against the wall, Charlotte wished she could just go home. Then she felt guilty, and selfish and pathetic for wanting to run away when Dotty and Mags had nowhere to run to. How lucky she was to even have somewhere to go!

She couldn't abandon Ben, either, but she wasn't going to uncover a saboteur in that mill, not when it was impossible to hold a conversation in there. If there was a plot to disrupt production, it would have to be discussed in the evenings, and no one seemed to have the energy to do that. And even if they did, no one would tell a new girl. She'd been so concerned about following Ben's plan, she hadn't stopped to consider if it was actually a good one.

It was hopeless, and she had to tell him so. Charlotte listened at the doors in the vain hope of hearing something, and then decided there must be another way in; surely there would have to be a door between the main mill and where the magi worked? For emergencies, if nothing else.

By the time she got back round to the worker's entrance to the mill, most people were returning to their looms. She saw Dotty wiping hers down and clearing lint, too absorbed to notice her go past and slip down the far side so she could get a better look at the wall between the mill and the magi's section. There was a door right at the far end, but without any legitimate reason to go through it as a mill worker, she stopped, frustrated.

"Oi!" The foreman's shout made her jump. "What are you up to?"

He was staring at her from the other end of the row of looms. With no good answer to give him, she hurried back to Dotty.

To Charlotte's dismay, the foreman was waiting by Dotty's looms when she arrived. "There ain't nothin' for you over there," he said. "What were you lookin' for?"

"Nothing, I—" The words died when she saw the thick leather strap he was holding. Charlotte had a horrible feeling she was about to find out what getting "a strapping" meant.

"She's new, Mr Foreman," Dotty said, a quiver in her voice. "She just got turned about in 'ere, that's all."

"I saw you sniffing about the other entrance," the foreman said. "'Opin' to catch someone's eye, were yer? There ain't no jobs 'ere for pretty things lookin' for rich husbands, I can tell yer that. Don't y'know them magi can't marry? Unless you were 'opin' to lift yer skirt for a bob or two?"

Charlotte gasped. "How dare you!"

The strap was raised and came down so quick that Charlotte had no hope of avoiding it. It hit her across her left arm and shoulder, sending her into the nearest loom and making a sharp pain explode through her hip where she hit the cast-iron upright.

"You're 'ere to work!" the foreman bellowed. "Not flutter yer eyelashes at some magus, 'opin' he'll let y'off a shift!" The strap whooshed through the air a second time, this time catching her forearms as she tried to defend herself.

The blow was hard enough to make tears come to her eyes. As the third came down, the bell rang and the shafts turned once again. Her sleeve caught on the loom's drive belt, snagging on a rough piece of leather that had patched up an earlier tear, and her arm shot up towards the line shaft with it. For a terrifying moment she felt her feet leave the floor, and then without even considering the consequences, Charlotte snapped the drive belt with a thought. She tumbled free, landing with her sleeve torn as the loom juddered to a halt.

The foreman's strap came down again, catching her across the head this time, as she was too shaken to defend herself. She couldn't hear the crack of it against her, the sound stolen by the din of the looms weaving again, but the pain was even more intense. She raised her arms again, but when the expected blow didn't come, her fear was rapidly replaced by rage. At the back of her mind, there was the faintest memory of one of her lessons with Hopkins.

"Your temper will be the end of you," he'd said. "Unchecked rage can turn a Latent wild, and it only takes a moment for control to be lost. That's why you need the marque."

Her marque was the furthest thing from her mind. She was going to wrench that strap from the foreman's hands and beat him to death with it.

Someone was screaming at a high enough pitch to rise above the clatter of the looms, and it snapped Charlotte from her murderous fury. It was Dotty, and for an awful moment she feared the foreman had turned on the poor girl for defending her. The foreman was nowhere near Dotty, though—he was still standing where he had been before, but now the strap was hanging from his hand at his side. Charlotte saw the wide-eyed terror on his face as he stared at something behind her.

She whipped her head round just in time to see the loom rise a couple of feet off the ground and then slam down again, making the floor shake. She scrabbled away on her backside as it rose a second time, only to buckle in the middle before being dropped again, as if a giant's invisible hand were squeezing it.

For one terrifying moment, Charlotte thought she was doing it, that she'd lost control like she had during Ben's test when she smashed a window and broke the dining room table. She tried to remember her marque, but the visualisation exercise was impossible when the loom's wooden frames were splintering apart right in front of her.

The shuttle had fallen to the floor, as had the roll of fabric collected at the side of the machine, and the broken threads were already a tangled mess. Half the frame lifted into the air again and Charlotte saw a wispy form above it, just for a moment, before the wood dropped to the floor and splintered into kindling.

Wondering if she'd imagined it, Charlotte stared at the air above the broken loom, but the violence seemed to be over. The foreman, visibly shaking, looked at her and Dotty and then beckoned to them to follow him out of the mill.

Dotty helped Charlotte to her feet, both of them shivering. With arms wrapped around each other, they went outside, Charlotte studiously avoiding making eye contact with the nearby workers. Even though those working the looms around them had seen it all happen, they still kept an eye on their own work. Now Charlotte knew why; they were keen to avoid a beating.

She wanted to cry. She could feel welts burning beneath her dress, her cheek was stinging where the end of the strap had caught it and her head throbbed. But she wouldn't give that man the satisfaction of seeing her upset. She gritted her teeth when she saw him outside, promising herself that she would tell Ben about him and see to it that he lost his job. It was the least she could do for Dotty.

"I don't want either of you t'say anything about what y'saw," he said, still gripping the strap. "None of it, d'yer 'ear?"

"But other people saw it too!" Charlotte said, and he scowled at her.

"*They* already know not to talk." His voice was more a growl. "Now get back in there and get on w'yer shift." He pointed the strap at Charlotte. "Any more wanderin' about and yer out. There's plenny more who'd give their eye teeth to work at this 'ere mill. I want t'see you workin' a loom by the end of today, else it's the cardin' room for yer and y'won't like that, either."

Dotty pulled at Charlotte's hand. "C'mon Charlie," she said timidly. "You can load the next empty shuttle, for practice."

Charlotte levelled an angry glare at the foreman and the strap twitched, making Dotty pull her harder. She let herself be guided back into the ovenlike mill, deafened once more, but more motivated to stay now. She didn't know what she had seen above the loom, nor whether it was even real. Whatever it was, she feared she'd started it off when she'd lost her temper.

Resolving to stick it out to the end of the shift, Charlotte made a mental list of grievances to take to Ben. He had to know what it was like here. He had to understand how badly the people were treated. And she had to keep her temper, or saboteurs would be the least of her brother's problems.

Chapter 5

BY THE END OF THE SHIFT, Charlotte was managing one of Dotty's looms whilst shadowing her on the others. The first time she'd had to change the shuttle, she'd been so terrified the loom would start up again whilst she was tying on the new thread. Dotty had taken pity on her and shown her, yet again, but Charlotte couldn't explain what she was really afraid of. If her hand were maimed, she'd never be able to draw again.

She was so tired after eating the measly soup and roll that she almost fell asleep at the dining table. She'd planned to ask Dotty about the other incidents, but then the sun was setting and she had to get to the cottage.

There were no rules about having to stay within the mill complex, but the gates were locked a few minutes after eleven bells. She walked as quickly as her aching legs allowed. She wasn't the only one heading out, to her relief. It felt strange, going out without a proper bonnet, so she'd tied her shawl under her chin, making her look like a washer woman. She didn't care. At least the red mark on her cheek was hidden.

There was a reassuring glow coming from the cottage's ground floor window as she approached. Ben opened the door before she'd even knocked. She stepped inside wordlessly and went into the small front room as he shut the door.

"Charlie?" he followed her in and watched her drop into the dusty armchair. "Have you no greeting for me?"

She glowered at him, making no effort to disguise her exhaustion. His eyes widened. "Good lord. You look terrible." He collected something from the hall and came back in. "I brought you some currant buns and a bottle of ginger beer. Here, I'll open it for you."

He passed her the opened bottle and she drained it so quickly it gave her indigestion.

"Charlie Bean, say something, dear. You're worrying me."

"You have sent me to work in hell."

His concerned frown warred with a nervous smile. "Come now, it can't be so bad."

"It's awful, Ben, truly awful."

He started to pace. "Well, you won't have to be there for long. Tell me, what have you learned? Any suspects?"

She stared at him. He had no idea. She wanted to shout at him, but couldn't find the energy to do so. She suppressed an uncomfortable belch, still thirsty. "No. There aren't any suspects. The poor souls who work there are too exhausted to organise any sabotage."

"I heard there was an incident today. Didn't you see anything?"

"I was there! And there were no other workers involved, I can tell you that. The loom lifted off the floor and smashed itself to pieces, without any help from your fictitious ringleader."

He paled. "I don't understand."

"It's as I say! I saw it with my own eyes. I was almost killed. Well, that was because the foreman knocked me into the loom and my sleeve caught on the strap and lifted me up."

"Good God, Charlie!" He knelt in front of her, seizing her arms. "You must be more careful!"

"You're hurting me!"

He was so strong now, and didn't seem to realise it. He let go quickly as if she were a dish pulled from the oven, too hot to touch. "I'm sorry. Tell me everything. What happened to the loom?"

She told him exactly what she saw, all except seeing the wisp above it. She wasn't sure what he'd make of that.

"And no one else was near to it?"

"Only the foreman. I was so furious with him, Ben, he—"

"You lost your temper?"

"Only for a moment. He—"

"Charlie! For the love of all that is good in this world, you must report yourself for testing! Don't you see? *You* made this happen!"

She shook her head. "No, that's not true," she said, trying to disguise her own doubt.

Still kneeling in front of her, he rested his hands on her knees. "Charlie, you can't hide this anymore. I know you love George and want to marry him, but don't you see how much danger you'd put him in? And even if you managed to keep yourself in check, what if you were reported after your wedding? He'd be prosecuted for hiding a Latent. That would be the end of his career, possibly his freedom. If you really do love him, you must submit yourself to the Royal Society!"

"It's under control." She forced herself to look him straight in the eye as she said it. "I would never put him at risk."

"If you don't do this yourself, darling, *I* will have to report you."

"No!" She pushed him away. "If you do that, I swear I'll . . . I'll throw myself off Tower Bridge!"

Appalled, he stared at her. "What a terrible thing to say!"

"I'd rather drown than be one of their prisoners!"

He stood up, running his hands through his hair. "Like I am?"

She studied his face. He was defensive, and she needed to be more cautious around him. He was one of theirs now. As much as she wanted to believe he would take her side over that of the Royal Society, she couldn't be certain. She blinked away the tears brought by that realisation. She was losing him. And from his point of view, she was being reckless; he had no idea about what Hopkins had been doing to help her. Of course, she couldn't tell him. She had to redirect the conversation.

"Dotty, my friend, said this happened before," she said. "In one of the previous incidents." It was only a small lie. If nothing like that had ever happened before, the foreman and Dotty would have been much more frightened by it.

"No one said anything to me about looms lifting into the air."

"Of course not," she said. "The foreman told us to keep quiet. I'm not supposed to tell a soul, otherwise he'll beat me again."

"Again?"

She'd never seen Ben look angry before. "He saw me looking at the wall that divides the mill from where the magi must be. It wasn't even when I was supposed to be at the looms; it was still in the lunch break. He hit me with the strap." She pulled the shawl down to show him the mark on her face. "There are other bruises, too."

Ben's face flushed scarlet. "As soon as I have the power to do so, I'll see to it that he's dismissed," he said through gritted teeth. "I'm so sorry, Charlie. I've put you in danger. What was I thinking? I'll never forgive myself."

The words flooded her with relief. He was still her brother, despite the gulf between them now. "I forgive you. You had no idea what it's like for the people who work there."

"They get three meals a day and a safe place to sleep," he said, folding his arms. "Ledbetter Mills are the best employers in the area." He actually looked proud of this. "The best in the country, I'd wager. Everyone wants to work there."

Now it was her turn to stare at him. "If that is one of the best mills, I dread to think what the worst ones are like."

"Oh, come now. You're simply not used to it, that's all. It's just a bit of a shock. Only another day or so and you can put it all behind you. Why are you looking at me that way? What have I said?"

Charlotte pressed her lips tight together, willing herself to stay calm. She shouldn't be angry with him. But she couldn't stand the way he looked at her, like she was some feeble girl who was overreacting. "I have no idea how you think I will be able to just put this behind me. How can I just go back to my life, leaving those poor souls in a place like that?"

"You're clearly overtired and upset about that dreadful foreman. There's no need to be so melodramatic!"

"Melodramatic!" She jumped to her feet, her exhaustion forgotten in her anger. "Those meals are not enough to keep a child's belly full, let alone an adult working a fifteen-hour day! And that's not to mention the heat and the air inside that place! And the noise . . . my ears are still ringing!"

"It's hard work, Charlie, you're just not used to it."

She took a breath to argue but the ringing in her ears got louder and the room started to darken. She was dimly aware of Ben guiding her back into the armchair and then, with the utmost embarrassment, Charlotte realised she'd almost fainted.

"I'll open the window," Ben said. "You look fit to pass out."

He didn't lift the net curtain to open the sash, keeping his face hidden from view. She realised he was afraid someone would see him there; it reminded her of the risk they were taking.

The fresh air helped. "I can't describe how awful it is for them there," she said, Ben kneeling in front of her again, this time looking at her with concern. "There are people with fingers missing . . ."

"That's because of the old type of looms, darling," he

said. "The new ones are a lot safer."

"And there are children with deformed legs . . ."

"If they didn't work at the mill, they'd work somewhere else," Ben said. "Sweet Charlie Bean, always wanting to take care of everyone. It isn't your fault they have to work. It's just the way things are for that sort of person."

"What do you mean?"

"They wouldn't be there if their parents had bettered themselves. Like ours did. Don't forget that our grandparents were dirt poor, living off the land. They came into the city and they worked hard and lifted their children up, do you see?"

She thought of Dotty. "Some of them don't even have parents."

"And that's sad, but—"

"And how can they better themselves when they can hardly stay awake at the end of a shift? Most of their wages goes to food and board, so how can they ever change their lives?"

Ben laughed. "You expect the mill to pay for their subsistence? Most mills pay less and leave the workers to find their own beds in the slums. Ledbetter's—"

"It's killing them, Ben! They look so ill and they cough all the time—it's the air, I'm sure of it—I've been coughing, too, and they won't let anyone open the windows! They're so cruel!"

He sighed. "That isn't cruelty! The air has to be warm and humid, otherwise the cotton threads snap! And if they opened the windows, the lint would fly about and make things worse."

She could understand the logic of that, but it still seemed cruel. And the thought of going back there in the morning, working those frightening machines, filled her with unspeakable dread.

"I don't think this was a good idea after all," he said, looking at her. "I shouldn't have made you do this. I feel terrible. I'll get your things and we'll put you up a hotel tonight and—"

The thought of a hotel bed was almost too tempting. But then she remembered why she had gone through that awful day at the mill. "No, Ben! We have to understand what's happening there. If you send me home, there's no way for you to beat Paxton. What if he pins it all on you?"

"It hardly seems decent to prioritise my apprenticeship over your safety."

Truth be told, she wasn't only thinking of that. She had to be certain she hadn't caused the loom's destruction, and if it hadn't been her doing, she had to understand what had happened! Besides, she was hoping to gather other evidence against Ledbetter. "Ben, I need to do this. As much as you love me, I love you. I won't let you down."

The clock towers rang out over the city, a different range and harmony to those of London, reminding her how far she was from home. Was Hopkins in one of those towers now? How she wished she could see him.

They looked at each other. "Nine bells. It's getting dark," Ben said. "I can't escort you back, though. I might be seen."

She stood, feeling better than before. "It's not far. May I take the currant buns with me?" At his nod, she picked up the bundle and went to open the door. She looked outside at the darkening street, hesitating.

"I'm sorry it's so hard, Charlie. Truly, I am."

"I'll be all right," she said, turning to look back on him in the shadows of the hallway. "I can go home soon. They can't. Darling, you must promise me that you will try to make things better there, as soon as you can."

"I promise," he said after a long pause. "Come back same time tomorrow. And be careful, Charlie."

When he closed the door behind her, Charlotte felt horribly alone. She wriggled her fingers between a gap in the brown paper and counted four buns. She allowed herself to pick one currant off the top before closing it up again, saving them for the ladies in her dorm. She felt Ben watching her as she left, so she looked back in the hope of one last wave, but there was only darkness at the windows.

Chapter 6

ON THE WAY BACK to the mill gates, Charlotte looked for Hopkins amongst the gentlemen going about their business. She searched the tide of dark grey and black frock coats, hoping for a glimpse of burgundy, but there was none.

She was disturbed by how disappointed she felt. When she'd collided with him in the street in the midst of the crisis with her father's debt, she'd been furious with him for his interference. Now she craved it. She felt jittery and unfocused, her heart a starling, fears blooming in her stomach. What if she had broken the loom? What if her grip on her abilities wasn't as secure as she'd thought? In London, at the end of her last lesson with Hopkins, he'd actually complimented her on it.

She'd beaten him in a game of bagatelle, having successfully controlled the small metal balls with enough finesse to move them around the wooden pegs and into the little holes on the board to score the highest points. None of the balls in play had been engraved with their respective marques, to make it fair. As a Fine Kinetics magus, Hopkins would have won hands down if the balls had been fully under his command. When they totted up the final scores and Charlotte was declared winner, she'd squeaked with delight.

"You could be one of the most powerful magi in the city," he'd said, with no little admiration. He so rarely complimented her, it had made her blush.

"Well, I have an excellent tutor."

"My dear Miss Gunn," he'd said with one of his devastating smiles. "Your power has nothing whatsoever to do with me. Your ability to control it, however, does. You do understand the risk we are taking, don't you?"

She'd nodded, solemn. "Won't you tell me what you have in mind for me, Magus Hopkins? You said that I'd be your eyes and ears, and that we'd take down Ledbetter together. When can we start?"

The way he'd looked at her then had made her feel most strange. It was as if he were reluctant, but there was something else in his eyes that she could not fathom. She found it hard to read him, distracted as she was by how unreasonably handsome he was. He'd gotten up and crossed the small garret where they always met, hidden at the top of the Henrietta Street clock tower. There was a small window that looked down over Covent Garden. Their lessons always took place against a backdrop of shouts from the vegetable and flower sellers. "Soon," he'd finally said, though she suspected that many other thoughts had gone unspoken. "Perhaps I have been overprotective." He'd twisted round sharply then. "Of the general public, you understand. Sending you out to investigate something, perhaps even using your esoteric skills, feels like sending a fishing boat laden with gunpowder out onto the Thames."

She'd deflated at the fact that he wasn't confessing to being overprotective of her, and had immediately felt another sharp pang of guilt. How absurdly selfish of her, to wish that he'd want to keep her safe for any other reason. She was engaged to be married to a man she loved dearly, one who loved her, too. George had a respectable job and an admirable character. Hopkins was a magus of the Royal Society, forbidden to marry, like a Catholic priest. She'd tried so hard to think of him that way, like a man of the cloth there to guide her, rising above thoughts of the flesh. It was almost impossible, when he had a face that could have been carved into marble and admired for all time. And those blond curls ... How many times had she sat on her hands to stop herself from discovering how it would feel to let them play through her fingers? And his lips ... How many times had she imagined how they would feel upon her skin?

Then she'd remembered what he'd said. "I am no fishing boat, sir!"

He'd laughed. "My apologies. A royal barge, perhaps."

"Oh, so I am wide and lumbering?" She'd stood, grabbing her bonnet and shoving it onto her head. "Thank you very much."

"It amuses me that you take offence to the type of vessel rather than the gunpowder," he'd said, with that maddening glint in his eyes. It was as if he enjoyed seeing her cross with him. What a perverted creature he was. How glad she was to be engaged to her sensible, kindly George.

She'd tied the ribbon of her bonnet so swiftly and with so little care that she caught a pinch of her skin in the bow. She'd ignored the sting, not wanting to show how he unsettled her. "Thank you for your lesson, Magus Hopkins," she'd said tersely. "I bid you good day."

"Don't forget to leave by the tunnel," he'd reminded her. As if she would forget! It was the only entrance she ever used. She couldn't be seen going into a clock tower in broad daylight!

"Do you think me entirely stupid?" she'd snapped, and then he was in front of the door, scooping up her hand as was his way, bending to kiss the back of her glove tenderly. She'd gritted her teeth as her toes curled inside her boots.

"Far from it, Miss Gunn," he'd said, finally releasing her. "Good day."

Charlotte was so absorbed in her memory of him that she almost bumped into a lady crossing her path. Stopping just in time, Charlotte said, "Oh, I do beg your pardon! My mind was quite elsewhere!"

"I could see that, love."

It was Mags, from the mill, and Charlotte blinked at her in surprise. "Oh, Mags, hello! Are you going back to the dorm?"

"I was 'opin' to speak to you first, lass, if y'don't mind? P'raps we could walk the long way round to our gate?"

Charlotte nodded, hearing something in the woman's voice that put her on edge. "Of course."

"What y'got there?" Mags nodded at the little bundle.

"Currant buns," Charlotte replied. "I thought we could share them out in the dorm."

"Well, there's a kindly thought," Mags said. "Did y'fancy fella give them to yer?"

Charlotte reddened. "I beg your pardon?"

"The bakery closed before the end of our shift, so y'couldn't 'ave bought them yerself." Mags, hands on hips, tilted her head as she examined Charlotte's face. "Who are you really, Miss Baker?"

"What do you mean?"

Mags scratched her chin. "I'm not the sorta woman who plays games. I like it all out in the open. I can't be arsed with tricks or with bloody bible bashers sendin' in their soft daughters to try and do God's work in t'mill."

"Bible basher? I have no idea what you're talking about." As she denied it, Charlotte tried desperately to think of a good excuse for the buns, but it was clear that was the last thing on Mags's mind.

"Who are yer? Who sent yer?"

"No one, don't be silly! I told you, my husband died and—"

"Oh, go on with yer. I've never 'eard such a load of bobbins in my life. There's no way you've lived through that. Look at yer. All fresh faced and plump cheeked. You've never 'ad to scrimp nor scrub to survive. Did that *Ben* send yer?"

The flush that crept up Charlotte's throat was enough to heat a small room. "Were you eavesdropping?"

Mags nodded. "I'll come clean. I followed you, cos I knew y'weren't what you said y'were. I wanted to know who sent yer. Who's that Ben? Did he send you t'work at t'mill?"

How much had she heard? For a moment, all Charlotte could do was steady her breath, panicked by the thought of what she and Ben had discussed. But then she remembered him opening the window late in the conversation. That might have saved her. Surely if Mags had heard anything about the Royal Society, this conversation would already be going very differently. There was no point denying it; she'd obviously heard enough to know that Charlotte was spying.

"Ben is my brother," she said, not wanting Mags to think

she was the kind of young lady who would sneak off to meet her lover in a seedy cottage, despite the fact that she was actually a young woman who regularly sneaked off to meet a magus. "He's not a 'bible basher.' He's a writer."

Mags nodded and the tension eased. "Ah, someone who wants to expose what life is like for us common folk, eh? But too high and mighty to do it 'imself? Or did you just draw the short straw?"

"No, it's not like that," Charlotte said, settling more comfortably into this lie, it being much closer to the truth. "I do the illustrations for him. In secret. He passes them off as his own. We've been working together for a couple of years now." It was easy to say, because it was what she'd always wanted as a child. She and Ben had talked about it as he lay in bed, sick, as life passed him by. Charlotte would read to him and they'd talk about him writing stories that she could illustrate. But he never had the energy to create anything, and as soon as he was well again, the last thing he wanted was to sit at a desk. "We want to expose how bad the conditions are in the mill." That was true, for her, at least.

Mags sighed. "Yer not the first, y'know. Listen to me, lass. It's clear you're a delicate one, and this ain't the place for yer. Y'need to go back to that brother of yours and tell 'im you've 'ad enough. There's no shame in it."

"No shame? I beg to differ. What sort of person would

I be if I ran away after only one day?"

"The sort of person who 'as somewhere to go," Mags said. "The only people who work in places like this are the ones who 'ave no choice."

Charlotte grasped Mags's arm. "But that's exactly the reason why I *must* stay! The people who don't have to work here simply don't care. And that's wrong."

Mags arched an eyebrow. "It's the way of the world, lass. In't that what yer brother said? For people like us?"

"Well, it shouldn't be," Charlotte said. "And anyway, what he said was thoughtless and rude and desperately unfair."

Mags smiled at her and rested her hand over Charlotte's. "Ee by 'eck, I knew you was more than you look!"

Charlotte couldn't understand the change in the woman's demeanour. "Have I missed something?"

Mags laughed. "I wanted to see if y'were goin' to give up, y'know, when I found you out. But yer not, are yer? There's a fire in y'belly, and y'might be a slip of nothin' but yer just the sorta person we need." She linked arms with Charlotte and they started walking again. "Thing is, love, there's been a few of us that's been tryin' to get people to pay attention for a long while. We've tried all sorts of things, but the magi are vicious sods, and they don't like anyone standin' up to 'em. I was lookin' out for yer because the last time someone got into t'mill to spy on workin' conditions, she got caught by the Royal Society, and it didn't go well for 'er."

Charlotte's blood chilled. "What happened to her?"

"She were transported. To Australia, y'know. They still do that, especially to thems that don't like the way the magi do things. So you think on, lass. If you and y'brother are really plannin' to write somethin' about this mill and 'ow things are, you might end up on one them ships, too, if yer not careful."

The thought of transportation was almost as frightening as being taken by the Royal Society's Enforcers. "We'll be careful. What did you mean about being the sort of person you need?"

"Like I said, me and a few others 'ave been tryin' to make things better for a while now, but no one listens to us. There are thousands like us who need work, and if we don't like it, the magi can tell us to bugger off and give our place to someone who won't complain. Ledbetter prides himself on givin' us food and beds, but you've seen what it's like. I 'eard what you said to y'brother and you were spot on; once yer 'ere, yer trapped. Once all the food and board and whatnot is paid for, you'll be lucky to have a shillin' a week spare. I've tried to organise savin' schemes for people, you know, savin' up to get out one day, but it's bloody hopeless. Most just want a bloody drink at the end of the day, and I can't say I blame 'em. We're supposed to feel lucky, when them magi and that bloody Ledbetter swan about in their fancy clothes, livin' out in t'country in their fancy houses, earnin' a fortune from our labour. Kids are crippled and we die young. It's not right."

Charlotte nodded earnestly. "I couldn't agree more."

"We need someone like you, someone who can bring the middle class on side. That's where we keep fallin' down, y'see. No one in parliament is goin' to listen to a bunch of buggers like us when they've got them rich magi tuckin' banknotes in their pockets and givin' 'em cigars, are they? But if nice young ladies like you went 'ome, spoke to yer friends who spoke to their 'usbands and they spoke to their bosses, well … well, maybe someone in Parliament might actually listen."

The more Mags said, the more Charlotte realised that there was more to the woman than she'd assumed. She wasn't talking like an unhappy employee—she was talking like someone who was part of a movement. Bringing the middle class on side? Only someone who saw a bigger picture than just the conditions in their own mill would say such a thing.

"Maybe," Charlotte said. "I'm going to do everything I can to draw attention to this, I promise. But please, don't tell anyone else who I really am."

"Of course I won't!" Mags said, squeezing her arm. "Though y'do stick out like an orange in a barrel full of apples. Nowt to be done about that, though."

"Something happened today, to one of the looms . . ."

Mags nodded. "Aye, I didn't see much, I were on t'other side. I 'eard y'got a strappin', though."

Charlotte tugged her shawl forwards, making sure the welt was covered. "The foreman is a horrible man."

"Better than the last one, believe me."

Charlotte tucked that grim thought away for later consideration. "He said I shouldn't talk about it with anyone, but I can't stop thinking about it. Mags . . . the loom . . . it lifted into the air. It smashed itself up!"

Mags nodded, eyes ahead as the street grew darker. They passed a man lighting the gas lamps, but it did little to make it feel safer. "Aye, I 'eard that, too."

"Has it happened before? What could cause that?"

Mags was silent as they rounded the corner to walk down the edge of the mill site. She looked behind her before speaking. "That's only 'appened the once, an' it's proof that things are gettin' worse. The first few times, the looms just crumpled up. When the foreman asked who did it, there were no one to blame, so he accused us of lyin' to protect the ones in charge of those looms. Then it 'appened again, and the foreman thought it were a conspiracy. Then last week, when that loom lifted up like that, the foreman saw it with his own eyes. He were right shaken up, and not just cos he realised we'd been tellin' the truth. He went to Ledbetter and told him what he saw, but Ledbetter said he were a socialist conspirator, as bad as the rest of us. He were found dead in t'gutter the next day. Drank himself to death, apparently. Bunch of arse, that is. That's why the foreman told yer to keep quiet. He'll do the same, see? He don't want to be 'drunk to death,' either, if y'know what I mean."

So Ledbetter had been told the truth and simply didn't believe it? Ben's socialist conspirators didn't even exist. But how could she persuade him of that, when he suspected it was her, turning wild? "Have you seen it happen?"

Mags nodded. "I were down the other end of a row when it 'appened last week. Killed a boy, it did. The loom landed on 'im, poor bugger."

Charlotte bit her lip. "That's awful."

"Aye. And nothin's bein' done about it, either. But then, short of gettin' a priest in, I'm not sure what could be done."

"What do you mean?"

They reached the gates and Mags stopped. "Well, it's obvious, in't it? Them looms weigh half a tonne. There's only two things that could lift them into the air, and the magi aren't goin' to do anythin' that risks their income, are they? So there's only one thing it could be. Ghosts."

Chapter 7

EVEN THOUGH SHE WAS so tired it felt like her body was weighed down with lead, Charlotte simply could not sleep. The currant buns had gone down well and several of the ladies who shared the dorm had warmed to her as they shared stories over the divided treats. Charlotte had stayed quiet, thinking over what Mags had said about the other incidents, and Ben's insistence that she submit for testing. The brother she loved so dearly was turning into the greatest threat to her freedom.

Now that she was in bed, she couldn't stop churning over the puzzle before her. Ben thought there was a saboteur, but having witnessed the loom's destruction, Charlotte knew that couldn't be true. However, his fear of there being some sort of socialist contingent at the mill might have some basis in fact, given the way Mags had talked. Charlotte had agreed with everything she'd said, though. Did that mean she was a socialist? Weren't they supposed to be bad people? It was all very confusing. Regardless, they weren't the cause of the problem. Neither was she, by the sound of it; the last incident had involved the loom being lifted into the air, long before she'd even reached the city. Her fragile confidence in her self-control remained intact.

Mags thought the loom had been destroyed by an angry ghost, and had delighted in trying to frighten them all with a scary tale before lights out. It had no impact on Charlotte; everyone knew there was no such thing. Gone were the days of ignorance, before the Royal Society had explained how supernatural activities could be more than adequately explained by the rise of latent magi. Indeed, reports of ghostly sightings had all but ended, now that Latents were rounded up and confined before their loss of control could be mistaken for poltergeists.

But she had seen something wispy in the air above the loom. Perhaps it was just some cotton fibres catching the light, and in her fearful state, her mind had made it into something more. That seemed eminently plausible, and the more Charlotte thought about it, the more she doubted what she saw. She'd been hit on the head, she was angry and frightened—how could she trust herself?

An alternative explanation was becoming more likely, one that made Charlotte feel awful: there had to be another Latent at the mill. For Mags the only explanation could be a ghost, but that was because she didn't believe that the Royal Society was fallible. Rogue Latents were always hunted down and contained. How could anyone be strong enough to destroy a loom and still be at large? Something that would be impossible in Mags's world was Charlotte's very existence. There had to be someone else at the mill hiding their abilities, or unable to accept that they were the cause.

There were many children there within the age range that abilities triggered. The only flaw in her theory was the fact they were still hidden. Surely if someone manifested esoteric ability, they would submit themselves for testing right away? It was a means of escape, not only from the mill, but also from poverty.

Perhaps someone else there shared her fear of the Royal Society. Maybe it was a child with no parents to watch over them and no idea what the strange events meant. But even then, the people they shared a dorm with and those who worked nearby would witness things. With such a generous reward for those who reported rogue Latents, it seemed unlikely that people would stay quiet. The only exception to that could be the foreman, separated from the staff as he was, but the fact that the former foreman had been found dead after reporting the incidents accurately eliminated him.

Charlotte didn't pretend to know everything about being a Latent, despite the fact she was one herself. Perhaps people manifested in different ways. Hopkins had made it clear she was exceptional—not just in terms of her power, but also the fact that she'd managed to stay hidden. She was certain that being a woman, often overlooked, was a great help. Perhaps that was also true for a poor mill worker, so ground into the dirt by life that no one could consider them exceptional, not even themselves?

The sound of the midnight bells made her sigh. She had to be up in four and a half hours. She rolled over and despite the coughing and snoring of her neighbours, Charlotte finally fell asleep.

• • •

The foreman pulled Charlotte and Dotty out of the flow of people entering the mill the next morning, and she braced herself for a dressing-down. Instead, the foreman simply asked if she was ready to take on four looms by herself if Dotty worked next to her. Charlotte agreed, relieved that nothing was said about the previous day's violence. The foreman beckoned for them to follow him inside, presumably to make sure that they were positioned next to each other, only to discover two people arguing in the same row.

Dotty hung back as the foreman strode over to tackle the dispute. "No one wants to work that loom," Dotty whispered. "It's been bashed up three times now."

"Do people usually work in the same places?"

Dotty nodded. "We all like to know where we are. People do change over sometimes, if someone's off sick, y'know, but mostly we're in the same place. The man who was next to us yesterday is usually down there, but after Bob . . ." She stopped, looking uncomfortable.

Charlotte pieced it together. "Did Bob die in the last incident? Was he the boy under the loom?"

"Oh, that were Sam," she said. "No, Bob was a loom worker, like us. He saw it lift into the air and keeled over in fright. They said it were his 'eart, but I dunno. No one wants to work that one now."

Charlotte approached the foreman. "I'll work that loom, if they don't want to," she said, indicating the one considered unlucky.

The foreman looked relieved, and shuffled the nearby workers around so that Dotty was stationed next to her. One of the men who'd refused to work it came over when the foreman's back was turned. "You mind 'ow y'go on that one," he whispered. "It's cursed. A boy and a man were killed there, and a girl lost a finger, too, so mind 'ow y'go."

Charlotte approached it with trepidation, checking that everything looked as it should. It was a new machine and looked quite pristine compared to its neighbours. After checking that there were shuttles loaded, ready to replace the empty ones when the time came, she waited for the bell to ring.

The tension built, as it had the morning before, as if everyone were holding their breath before being plunged into the frenetic working day. She dreaded the bell already, and the awful noise and heat that would soon follow. She was nervous too. Would she be able to manage the looms and keep an eye out for a possible Latent? And what should she do even if she discovered who it was? She'd already decided to speak to them first, rather than just turning them in. She'd help them as much as she could.

People started looking at each other, exchanging shrugs as the bell failed to ring. Dotty drifted closer, keeping an eye out for the foreman, to whisper to Charlotte. "The belts should be goin' by now. Do you think they're goin' to close the mill because of what 'appened?"

Charlotte shrugged, deeply worried by the prospect. Was Ben in charge today, or his rival? She hoped it was the latter, and that his production scores would be going down, not her brother's. Then she started to worry that someone had discovered what Ben was doing, and had collared him, stopping him from being able to work the line shaft. She chewed her thumbnail, quietly fretting, until she heard Dotty groan.

"Oh, no," she whispered. "Paxton's on the prowl. Look busy!"

Charlotte grabbed the cloth and started wiping down the frame of the nearest loom as the apprentice's fine boots clipped across the floor. She didn't dare look round, for fear that he would see a resemblance to Ben in her features; they had very similar brown eyes, after all.

"It were down this row, Master Apprentice Paxton," she heard the foreman say. Just the sound of that man's voice set her teeth on edge.

He was leading Paxton down the neighbouring row to the gap where the destroyed loom had stood the day before. She knelt in front of her loom, pretending to check the positioning of the partially filled roll of fabric, to avoid being seen across the way.

"These are very serious claims being made," said a deep, gruff voice. Paxton, she assumed, had an East End London accent, one familiar to her ear. He sounded like the dock workers she used to overhear on the streets near her old house when they were on their way back from trips into the centre of the city with their lady friends.

"And I wouldn't 'ave made 'em, if I didn't think it were serious," the foreman said. "I were up all night thinkin' about it. But I can't in good conscience manage a factory and not report goings on like that. P'raps that's why

Jimmy drank himself to death. It must 'ave scared the life out of him."

"I knew it," she heard Paxton mutter. "There's a rogue Latent on your staff, Foreman. Someone turnin' wild. Maybe someone who's got certain political sympathies. Who was workin' this loom yesterday?"

"There were two of 'em, Master Apprentice, two girls."

"Bring 'em over."

Charlotte, still huddled out of sight, looked across to Dotty who was busily polishing her machine, oblivious. Of course, she hadn't heard the conversation. She flapped her hand and Dotty looked over, frowning at the sight of Charlotte's panicked expression. She only had time to point in the direction of the foreman before he appeared at the end of their row.

"You two, come w'me," he barked.

There was nothing to do but obey. Charlotte didn't want to get another strapping, and if she ran now, she'd all but out herself as a Latent. Dotty grabbed her hand as they followed the foreman, giving a quick, reassuring squeeze before letting go.

As much as she wanted to stare at Paxton and get a good look at his face, Charlotte kept her eyes on his boots. They were well polished. She hoped he couldn't see how much she was shaking.

"The foreman has told me that the loom that was there

yesterday lifted into the air and smashed itself up. He tells me you two were there. That right?"

Charlotte nodded and saw Dotty do the same from the corner of her eye.

"Way I see it," Paxton said, taking a step closer, "this is either a load of codswallop, cooked up between yah to cover for some saboteurs, or one of yah is a Latent."

"Why one of us two?" Charlotte blurted. "There were dozens of other people nearby!"

"Who are you?"

"She's just a new girl," the foreman said. "She weren't working 'ere when the other loom . . . went funny last week."

"But she was?" He pointed at Dotty.

"Aye. That's Dorothy. She's been 'ere for a few years now. Longer than I 'ave."

"She were next to the loom that got smashed up last week!" said a man further down the row.

"I were not!" Dotty said. "I were over on t'other side, tell 'im, Mr Foreman!"

The foreman scratched the back of his neck. "I don't rightly recall," he muttered. "But she were definitely there yesterday, she were supposed to be lookin' after this loom."

"Right," Paxton said, grabbing Dotty's collar. "You're comin' with me."

Charlotte glared at the foreman as Dotty was pulled out of the mill. "You know she's got nothing to do with this! Tell him he has the wrong person!"

"Know who it was, do yer?"

She shook her head. "No, but it definitely wasn't Dotty! Why would she risk her job? She has nowhere else to go! If she was a Latent she'd have put herself forwards for testing to get out of this horrible place!"

The foreman looked briefly uncertain and then settled into a scowl. "Any more lip from you and I'll give y'another strappin'. You watch 'er looms when the shift starts."

"But I can't manage twelve!"

"I'll find someone to 'elp." He looked at the other workers, all watching. "What are you lot starin' at? That bell is gonna ring any moment now and we've time to make up. I'll take it out of yer lunch break if I see anyone slackin'!"

Charlotte watched Paxton pull Dotty through the double doors. Stupid man. He was so desperate to find a scapegoat, he wasn't even bothering to properly investigate.

Then she remembered what Hopkins had told her about people taken by the Enforcers who refused to co-operate. He'd implied that they were tortured. What if Paxton said she was a Latent and when she didn't show any ability, he thought she was being obstructive? Would he take it that far?

She looked around at the other workers, seeking any signs of guilt or relief at this turn of events. Everyone just looked scared, heads down, trying not to draw attention to themselves. All except Mags. She looked furious. Their eyes met and they shared a moment of pure frustration before the bell rang.

As the line shafts started to turn, Charlotte knew she had to do something. She had to prove that Dotty was innocent and definitely not a Latent, and the only way to do that was to have another "incident" when she wasn't in the mill. How could Dotty be guilty if it happened when she wasn't even there?

Looking around at the other people working the nearest looms, she saw how diligently they attended to their machines, not daring to draw any attention. Even Mags was minding the machines under her care, despite the stern frown still on her face. The foreman had gone off to find someone else to help her, and none of the children were nearby, either. It was now or never.

Charlotte pretended to drop her cloth so she could check that there was no child beneath the loom that everyone thought was cursed. Seeing it was clear, she stood at the loom farthest away that was under her care and pretended to watch the shuttle.

She thought of the "cursed" loom, reaching out for it with her mind, just as she had with the little ball bearings when she'd played bagatelle with Hopkins. She imagined the wooden frames clattering up and down, its shuttle whipping left to right, and then she imagined crushing it, drawing it all inwards to an imagined central point just below the machine.

A surreptitious glance told her some of the yarns had snapped, their ends flying around, caught in the eddies of air around the loom. Charlotte realised she was holding herself back, having spent months constantly reining herself in, always vigilant for any urge to lash out. Now she actually *wanted* to destroy something, it was proving harder than she imagined it would be.

She redoubled her efforts, thinking not just of the loom, but also Dotty and the way Paxton had just dragged her off. There was a cracking sound, loud enough to be heard over the rattling din of the machines, and she saw one of the other workers running away.

Charlotte had a proper mental grip on the loom, the sweat now running down her back caused by the exertion of her will to lift it into the air. She gripped the sides of the loom she stood in front of, steadying herself as the effort to destroy the other one stole the strength from her legs. A crash and a brief, violent tremor through the floor told her she'd done it.

Panting for breath, she watched the foreman return with the worker who'd run off. As others gathered round the mangled machine, Charlotte forced herself to move to the edge of the small crowd so she would blend in. She didn't have to fake her shock when she saw the loom. She'd never deliberately destroyed something before.

Something inside her exalted at the sight of what she'd done. Charlotte couldn't help but think of the dozens of threads strung over the frames of the looms around her and how easy it would be to break them too. She saw a couple snap on the machine next to her and squeezed her eyes shut, trying to pull her mind inwards. With a supreme effort, she managed to visualise her marque in the dark space behind her eyes, tracing the curves and swirling shape of the sigil, imagining it as a path she was walking with her mind.

As Charlotte started to sense her power retreating, the horror of what she'd just done hit her. It was exactly what she'd sworn she'd never do. Hopkins had warned her so many times. And even now, even when she was feeling more in control again, she could still feel a pull towards unleashing it once more. There was something inside her, desperate to be free. She clenched her fists, focused on her marque and tried not to think of anything else.

She felt the air move as someone passed her and she opened her eyes to see the foreman running towards the exit. Needing to get away from the looms herself, she followed him outside to find him bent over, hands braced on his knees.

"Where's Apprentice Paxton?" she asked.

"That's *Master* Apprentice Paxton to you," he fired back with a quiver in his voice.

"He needs to know what just happened," she said. "Dotty can't possibly be the Latent, can she?"

The foreman straightened. "No, I suppose not." He narrowed his eyes at her. "I don't like the way you're lookin' at me, lass. I've a good mind to get rid of yer. Y'don't fit in."

Charlotte saw his hand twitch towards the strap hanging from his belt and felt the edge of that raw power within her again. It would be so easy to just flick him across the yard, smash him against the wall . . .

No. She backed away, looking down, focusing inwards again. "I'll get back to my looms," she said. "Unless you want me to find Master Apprentice Paxton for you?"

It was a risky bluff, but she had to remind the irritating man that Dotty needed to be vindicated. "No, go on with yer. I'll see to that. I'd rather 'ave Dotty back than find a replacement at this hour. Go on! Get back in there and do some bloody work!"

Walking back into the mill felt like climbing a steep hill with a basket of washing on her back. Her body felt leaden and the sun hadn't even fully risen yet. Charlotte wanted to find some corner to hide in, somewhere to bundle herself up in blankets and shut out the world, just so she could be certain she was fully in control again. She couldn't understand why she was so tired when only minutes before, she'd felt invincible. But then the very thought of being in that state started to rejuvenate her, and she paused just inside the doorway to visualise her marque once more.

It was the act of reining herself in, of suppressing the power inside her, that was exhausting. She covered her face with her hands as she leant against the closed doors, fearing that she wouldn't be able to make it through the day. It felt like she'd released a ferocious beast from a cage it had been trapped in for years, and it was understand-ably reluctant to return to its confinement. She needed Hopkins, needed him to help her force the creature back into its prison. Then the most awful thought occurred to her: Why? Why deny such a fundamental part of herself? It took Charlotte a good few moments to realise it was to protect others. A choked sob escaped into her hands. Was she turning wild?

Chapter 8

WITHIN THE HOUR, Charlotte and Dotty were working the looms again, side by side. Every now and again Dotty would glance over at her, giving a shy, thankful smile. Charlotte could only assume the foreman had mentioned the way she'd pressed him to argue for her innocence. Dotty would never know the full extent of her intervention. Hopefully.

Paxton was still actively hunting for a Latent, though, and the thought made Charlotte want to run out of that mill and never return. The faster she could work out who was behind the previous incidents, the faster she could leave. But how could she find another Latent who was evidently hiding their ability as much as she was?

The broken loom was taken away, and she tried her best to put it from her mind. She focused on her work, hoping that the repetitive and boring tasks would restore her mental calm. Strangely enough, it did help, and soon she just felt hot and fatigued rather than feeling the pressure to keep herself under control. It seemed that the inner beast, as she'd come to think of it, was indeed back in its cage.

Working the looms was still nerve-racking, but she was becoming more confident by the hour. She even started to appreciate their design. She could understand how the different parts worked in concert and found herself starting to memorise the mechanism so that she might sketch it for Hopkins. She suspected he might be interested to see the machines that were making a fortune for his rival.

Her close inspection revealed a set of symbols engraved into the metal cogs at the side of the loom. They reminded her of the ones she'd seen on the mechanism hidden beneath the debtor's cage in London, but she couldn't find Ledbetter's marque amongst them. As discretely as she could, Charlotte looked for them on each of the looms she managed and discovered the same ones were on each machine in exactly the same places.

What could they be for? As far as she could tell, the only parts of the factory that would require magical operation were the huge line shafts running along the ceiling, and that fit perfectly with the skills of the Dynamics college. The symbols on the cogs would make sense if they were operated by a Fine Kinetics magus, but that would be impossible here; the mills were famously within the sole province of the Dynamics college. Charlotte studied the symbols as best she could, committing them to memory. Hopkins would be able to explain them.

When the bell rang for lunch and the clatter of the looms came to a stop, Charlotte noticed more symbols embossed into the leather drive belt. She looked as closely as she could without making it obvious, but Dotty was already encouraging her to get some food.

This time Charlotte had no trouble eating everything on her plate, but she still gave Dotty her bread roll, unable to bear the disappointment on her friend's face.

"Ta." Dotty grinned. "All that excitement 'as worked up an appetite!"

"Paxton didn't hurt you, did he?"

"No, he were just a bit rough. He took me round to where the magi are. It's right nice in there. The floor is all shiny like. He said he were gonna bring the Enforcers and that they'd do 'orrible things to me if I tried to hide my power. I don't think he's right in the 'ead. I told him that if I were a magus, I'd take meself off for testin' quick as lightnin'. Then he started sayin' that if I weren't a magus, I must be a socialist. I dunno what he was goin' on about. But then the foreman came and said it had 'appened again, so it couldn't be me. Paxton didn't look too 'appy about it, truth be told. I don't think he likes me."

"I think he just wanted someone to blame," Charlotte replied.

"Aye. At least he didn't throw me out. And you're gettin' the 'ang of the looms now. Y'need to speed up, though. The littl'uns know they 'ave to be quick. By the time you've crouched down to see if they're still tying a thread they've already moved onto the next loom."

Charlotte nodded. "I know. I just couldn't bear it if one of them got hurt because I started it too soon."

Dotty gave her an affectionate nudge with her shoulder. "You're a soft bugger, you are."

Keen to sketch the symbols from the looms whilst they were still fresh in her mind, Charlotte excused herself with a mention of popping back to the dorm, promising to see Dotty back in the mill. She hurried up the stairs and went straight there. Mercifully, it was empty. She pulled her sketchbook and pencil out from its hiding place between the frame and straw mattress, checked once behind her as she settled into a spot between the wall and her bed and got to work.

It didn't take long to draw them as they were fairly simple in design, and once they were done, she tore the page out, folded it and stuffed it between her corset and underdress to rest over her heart. It was one thing to risk having an empty sketchbook found, quite another for it to contain something esoteric.

She had to find Hopkins, but she couldn't imagine where to start, short of walking up to the local Fine Kinetic Arts college, or the Manchester branch of the Royal

Society. Neither were remotely advisable. As she went back down the stairs and back outside again, she remembered him mentioning something about the Reform Club commissioning a clock tower. Could that be a way to find him? Clubs were usually the province of wealthy gentlemen. If she turned up on the doorstep, asking for a magus . . .

Someone grabbed her as she passed the gap between the lodging house and the mill, dragging her round the corner. Before she'd even had a chance to cry out, Charlotte was slammed against the wall by one of the mill workers. His greying hair hung in limp, greasy waves and his two front teeth were missing, like so many of the others. Having bashed her own teeth on the shuttles when sucking the thread through the hole on the end, Charlotte understood why.

"I know you did it," he said, breath stinking of the cheap meat they'd just eaten.

"Did what?" Charlotte asked, drawing her arms inwards, making herself as small as possible as he planted his hands on either side of her shoulders, boxing her in against the wall.

"Wrecked that loom this mornin'. I were watching yer. I clocked yer as soon as y'started 'ere. Knew you weren't right. You're one of them Latents, aren't yer? That why you 'ere? Running away from the Enforcers are yer?"

"Why on earth would you imagine I'd prefer a mill to the Royal Society?"

He shrugged. "I dunno. Don't know yer. But I know what I saw this mornin', when yer little friend were dragged out by that magus. I saw you lookin' at that loom and then sweating even before bell went."

Charlotte could feel her lunch rising. "I was told it was cursed, of course I was looking at it."

"Ah, but them others, they don't notice things like I do. Otherwise they'd be 'avin' a very similar conversation with y'now. See, it ain't nothin' to do with bein' cursed. This mornin', no one were near that loom when it started smashin' up. All the other times, someone had hurt 'emselves on the machine before the smashin' started. So I know it were you."

In providing his evidence, he'd inadvertently put Charlotte's lingering fears to rest. When the foreman had hit her the day before, he'd knocked her into the loom, giving her the horrible bruise on her hip. Was pain somehow the trigger? Was it something the other Latent couldn't bear to see, triggering a violent reaction to the loom that caused it?

"Y'can't deny it, can yer?" he said, thinking hers was a guilty silence.

"I'm not listening to a moment more of this nonsense." She tried to sound dismissive but her voice was strained and her cheeks were blushing.

When she tried to duck under his arms he simply moved them, keeping her trapped. "Listening to yer, I reckon you've got money somewhere. I reckon y'doin' someone a favour, comin' 'ere. I reckon there's lots of folk who'd like to see this mill go down. Cartwright's company for a start. Are they payin' yer to ruin Ledbetter?"

"No," she said. "I'm not a Latent and I'm not working for anyone else."

"I don't believe yer." He leaned closer, forcing her to turn her face away. "And if y'don't give me . . . let's say, a nice shiny sovereign by light's out tonight, I'm gonna report yer to Paxton."

A sovereign? That was more than the cost of the coal bill for a month! As upsetting as it was to be blackmailed, the fact he wasn't already marching her off to be tested proved he had doubts. His fear of being fined for false reporting currently outweighed his desire to collect the finder's fee. Charlotte feared that if she pointed that out, however, his pride could tip him over into taking that risk anyway. "A sovereign? I don't have that kind of money!"

"Well, that ain't my problem, is it now? I'll meet you at the back of your lodgin' 'ouse at eleven bells. If you're not there, I'll report yer. If y'come empty-'anded . . . well . . ." He looked down at her bosom and licked his lips. "We'll 'ave a conversation about alternative means of payment."

"You disgusting man," Charlotte hissed.

"What's goin' on?" Mags was standing at the corner of the building, arms folded, scowling at the man. "You leave her alone, Horcombe, she's a good lass."

He stepped back, dropping his hands to his sides. "Nowt to see 'ere, Mags," he said. "Just wanted to make sure this new girl understands 'ow things work 'ere."

"Bugger off and tell that son of yours how things work, why don't yer?" Mags said. "Look after y'own instead."

Horcombe gave Charlotte a lingering look. "Nice talkin' to yer, miss."

Mags watched him go and came over to Charlotte who couldn't stop shaking. "What did he say? You're in a right state!"

Charlotte couldn't tell her the truth, but feared that if she lied and Mags challenged him, it would expose her deceit. So she just shook her head and smoothed down her dress, trying her best to compose herself. "It was just a misunderstanding," she said. "We have to go inside, it's nearly time for the bell."

Mags was frowning at her. "You tell me if he does anythin' dodgy and I'll give 'im what for, a'right?"

Charlotte nodded and managed a grateful smile, despite the fact that she was silently panicking. Now there was even more reason to leave, but she still couldn't bring herself to do it. If she ran away, and Paxton managed to outwit her brother, she would never forgive herself.

She had to find the other Latent responsible for the previous incidents, and fast. Whether it was by Paxton's or Horcombe's hand, if she was exposed as a Latent, Ben would end up in even more trouble.

. . .

At the end of the shift, Charlotte just wanted to collapse in a heap on the cobbles outside. The day had felt as long as a week. Dotty linked arms with her and steered her towards the water pump at the back of the lodging house. They ended up lined against the wall with other women, slumped, waiting for a turn at the pump to douse their heads in cold water.

It felt like someone had wrung her out. Charlotte had never experienced anything like it. She'd thought she was tired the day before, but she didn't even know the meaning of the word before now. She ended up sitting on the dirt, unable to stay standing as she waited. Even just shuffling along as the line dwindled was an effort. Dotty sat next to her and they ended up leaning against each other. By the time they got to the pump, the bell for dinner had already rung.

This time, Charlotte had just as much difficulty working the pump as Dotty had had on the first day. She almost wept with exhaustion as Dotty washed. The water helped a little when it was her turn, but it soaked her dress and she was so worried that it would wick through to the paper hidden beneath, she decided to skip dinner to change her clothes. She was too tired to eat anyway. Charlotte made sure she collected her bowl and roll so she could give them to Dotty—who kissed her on the cheek for her trouble—and went back to the dorm.

The prospect of walking to the cottage afterwards made her feel utterly miserable, but she had to tell Ben about Horcombe's threat. She couldn't see any other way around it. But how was she going to explain why she was being blackmailed without admitting she'd used her esoteric ability to destroy a loom? It was making her feel sick with nerves.

Yawning, Charlotte arrived at the dorm and headed in, only to realise that the woman she'd seen on the first night was lying on her bed again, with her back to the door. Charlotte sighed. She was too tired for this. "Excuse me, that's my bed now."

The woman coughed, sounding dreadfully ill. Charlotte hung back, unwilling to get close. "But I'm so tired," the woman whispered. "Just a little longer, please?"

Charlotte felt a pang of guilt and went over to sit on Dotty's bed. The woman didn't roll over at the sound of the bed's squeak. "Which one is your dorm?" she asked.

"Maybe it's the floor above. I got muddled up here the first day." Met with silence, Charlotte decided to start getting changed anyway. With the woman's back to her it was easy to take out the piece of paper and tuck it under Dotty's pillow as she unbuttoned her overdress.

"I'm so tired," the woman said again.

"Me too," Charlotte said. "Do you work the looms or do you do something else?"

"The looms," the woman replied. "Always the looms. I just want to sleep but they won't stop screamin.'"

Now just in her underdress and corset, Charlotte froze. "Screaming? Who?"

"Can't you 'ear them?"

She listened. There was the background hum of the city, with its carriages and sheer mass of people, but no screaming. "I can't. Was this earlier?"

"It never stops." The woman groaned.

Charlotte feared the poor woman was feebleminded, but then thought about how her ears were still ringing. "Oh, I can hear a high-pitched sort of ringing noise. It fades after a little while." She wondered if that was just because she hadn't worked there for very long. She'd noticed how loudly most people talked, as if they were all partially deaf. The woman didn't reply so Charlotte carried on getting changed. "What's your name?"

"Betty." The woman coughed again with an awful rattling wheeze lingering afterwards. "Oh, I just want to sleep but they won't stop screamin.'"

"I'm sorry, I can't hear them."

"I tried to tell 'em to be quiet, but they won't listen. It never stops."

Charlotte did up her buttons and stuffed the piece of paper back into its hiding place. She yawned. "Well, if you tell me where they are, I can go and speak to them." She fully expected Betty to say they were in the room with them, or nearby, thus proving her theory about her hearing.

"They're in t'mill."

A chill passed through Charlotte's body. "The mill?"

She went over to the window and opened it, leaning out to listen intently. There were no windows on the wall facing the lodging house, so she couldn't see inside, but she knew it would be empty in there now. Everyone was still at dinner.

So who was screaming in the mill?

Gripping the windowsill, Charlotte listened to what sounded like dozens and dozens of people screeching. It was a terrifying sound, as if they were being rent apart, and she slammed the window shut.

"Gettin' some fresh air, love?"

Charlotte yelped at the sound of Mags's voice and spun round. "Oh, Mags," she said, hand pressed over her chest to try to steady herself. "I heard them!"

"Who? Oh, pet, you're white as a sheet."

"The people that Betty"—Charlotte looked down at her empty bed—"that Betty told me about."

Mags looked at the bed. "Betty? But . . . Betty died last week, love."

Charlotte realised why the bed had been free when she arrived. She shook her head. "It must have been someone else," she said, but even she didn't believe that.

"She died there. She 'ad the cough really bad," Mags said. "Did y'really see 'er?" She took a step closer. "Did yer? I always knew there was such a thing as ghosts!"

"I . . . I made a mistake," Charlotte said, heading for the door. "I'll be back later." She ran from the room and didn't look back.

Chapter 9

CHARLOTTE WALKED AWAY FROM the lodging house briskly, in the hope that leaving that place behind faster would make what she'd seen less real. Unsteady, she stumbled on the uneven cobbles enough times to make her ankles ache, but she didn't slow down.

Ghosts? She didn't believe in ghosts. Nobody did. At least, nobody sane.

A boy crashed into her on the way to the cottage, snapping her mind back into her body again. He pressed a note into her hand before running off.

You are being followed. Take the next right and immediate left. Get to the far end of the alley as quick as you can.

It was from Hopkins! Charlotte set off again, even faster, even though it felt as if the shivering and fluttering panic riddling her body could shake it apart. She followed the directions, found the alley and ran through it, seeing a black Clarence carriage at the far end. The door opened as she approached, and the steps were kicked down. A gloved hand with a burgundy cuff reached down and pulled her up. By the time she was seated, the steps had been pulled back in, the door slammed and the command given to drive on.

Seeing Hopkins, blond curls free of a top hat and looking so divine in such a beautifully appointed carriage, made Charlotte feel like little more than a smudge on the corner of his page. She was shaking so violently that her teeth chattered. She wrapped her arms around herself, feeling like she had to physically hold herself together.

His usually placid demeanour faded quickly as he took in the sight of her. "Miss Gunn," he said, leaning forwards. "My goodness, are you quite well?"

"Do you believe in ghosts, Magus Hopkins?" Her voice wobbled as she spoke, as if she'd been standing outside in December without a coat, despite the warmth of the evening.

"Why do you ask?"

"Because I have just had a conversation with one." She laughed. It sounded so ridiculous. She clamped her hand over her mouth. She must appear quite mad.

His brow descended into a frown. "Miss Gunn, I think I should take you to my hotel. I think you need rest and a good meal."

"No, Ben is waiting for me. He'll be worried as it is." Not to mention the fact that going to his hotel room seemed desperately inappropriate, no matter how much she craved comfort and a warm bath. She mirrored his frown. "You don't believe me? Do you think I'm just tired and hungry?"

"No, I just think that being tired and hungry may be contributing to your distress. Tell me what happened."

She told him about Betty, about how she'd seen her the first night, about the conversation earlier and the sounds coming from the mill. As she described it all, Hopkins listened in attentive silence, and she could tell he believed her. And what was more, he was most concerned.

"It must have been very frightening," he said softly when she was done.

Tearful, Charlotte nodded, wishing that he would just gather her into his arms and steady her somehow. No, not him—George, of course. But he was so far away. "It's been the most beastly two days. How did you find me?"

"I followed you from the station. Please forgive me. I had to be sure you were safe. It was quite a shock to see you leave that cottage dressed as a mill girl."

"You must have watched us for hours!"

"Not every moment, my dear. I took tea when you did, I ate when you did, and I moved between locations a little way behind. I was otherwise quite absorbed in my reading materials. I had hoped to send you a note yesterday, to ensure your well-being, but I was invited to the most appalling play at the Theatre Royal by the head of my college here. I couldn't refuse. I've been quite worried about you, Miss Gunn, and it seems I was right to be."

She didn't have the energy to be irritated by the way he'd followed her—besides, how many times had she wished for him to appear? She had no right to be both disappointed in his absence during the past two days and irked by his nosiness. As she looked at him now, at the worry in his eyes, she realised he hadn't been nosy at all. He'd wanted to watch over her. His angelic guardianship made her burst into tears. "Oh, Magus Hopkins, it's so awful! So awful!"

Sobbing, Charlotte poured out everything that had happened, from the shock of the terrible working conditions to the blackmail, even confessing how hard it had been to rein herself back in after destroying the loom. Throughout, she feared she was telling him too much, but she was far too tired and upset to judge. It was all too tangled to separate out into the acceptable and the inadmissible and besides, she needed to tell someone who would understand.

He pulled a blanket from a box under the seat, moved across to sit next to her and draped it around her shoulders as she confided in him. She didn't think about how he stayed by her side, nor how he pulled off his gloves to rest his hand over hers as they clutched the blanket. When she finally stopped, everything confessed, she realised his hand was still there. His face was so close, she dared not turn to face him, lest their lips touch.

"My apologies, Miss Gunn," he said, hurriedly moving across the gap to return to his seat. "You were shivering."

She wiped her cheeks with her hand before accepting his handkerchief, passed across without comment. "I'm so terribly sorry. I don't know what came over me. I'm not in the habit of falling apart, especially in company."

"My dear Miss Gunn." Hopkins sighed. "There is no need to apologise. The only individual upon whom that obligation rests is your brother. What was he thinking, putting you in this position, knowing of your talents?"

"He was thinking about transportation, and avoiding it at all costs." Charlotte sniffed. "And I still want to help him. But I'm frightened. I don't want to go back to that place. Am I going mad, Magus Hopkins?"

"No," he said, unable to maintain his steady gaze. He reached for his gloves, lining them up to rest them on his knee and smooth them flat.

"What are you afraid to say to me?"

"You're not going mad," he said. "But I fear you are turning wild."

She bit her lower lip to stop it from trembling. "But I controlled myself. It was hard, I confess, but I did it."

"That's only part of turning wild." He leaned back, raking a hand through his curls, the most uncomfortable she'd ever seen him. Only now did she appreciate how studied his usual composure was. His eyes, so pale in the interior shade of the Clarence, looked deeper, somehow. Distressed. She clutched the blanket more tightly.

After silent deliberation, Hopkins knocked on the roof and consulted the driver briefly. "We're going to the edge of the city," he said to her.

"No, we can't. Ben is waiting for me, I told you!"

"It isn't far. We need to speak somewhere safe and there is no such place in the city. Besides," he added, "your brother deserves to worry. Putting you in this situation..." He shook his head as he fell silent, although she had the impression he could have spoken far more on the subject.

Hopkins was angry with Ben, and it made a spark flare in her breast. He was angry on her behalf. He cared about her. His glances, the pinched skin between his eyes, all confirmed it as the carriage raced along. She closed her eyes, trying to centre herself again and find the core of calm that she relied upon when her mother was getting hysterical. She thought of George, consciously trying to push the presence of Hopkins away from her mind and utterly failing to do so. She wanted him to come back over to the same seat as her, wrap his arms around her, hold her until she felt safe again.

She was a wicked woman and she didn't deserve George. Charlotte wiped away a new tear and wished that the blinds at the carriage windows were open so she had something to look at other than Hopkins.

"All will be well," he said, misinterpreting her fretful face. "You've had a terrible fright, off the back of two very trying days. You're coping magnificently. We'll talk this through, I'll look at those symbols you mentioned and we will make a plan. You are not alone in this."

His kindness made that spark burn all the more brightly. "Magus Hopkins?" she said hesitantly.

"Yes, Miss Gunn?"

"I think you . . ." She suppressed the words that rose to follow. ". . . are very kind and I thank you."

The road had become horribly bumpy all of a sudden and soon the carriage drew to a stop. He peeped out from behind the blind first and then, satisfied, opened the door, flipped down the steps and descended to help her out.

They were out in the open countryside. It was so disorienting after being in the city. It felt like she'd been in Manchester far longer than two days. The carriage had pulled off the main road, then down a small track to pull into a passing place so they wouldn't obstruct any carts returning to farms from the city.

Hopkins pulled a second blanket from the carriage and climbed over a gate into a nearby field. He found a spot free of sheep dung, spread the blanket out and sat down upon it. He patted a space on the blanket next to him and Charlotte sat down, feeling rather odd. It was like the preamble to a romantic picnic, only without the hamper. And the right man.

"This is going to be a difficult conversation," he said, pulling a long stalk of grass from its root to let it play between his fingers. He was nervous.

She reached into her dress and pulled out the piece of paper, but when she held it out to him, he pushed it back gently. "We'll come to that. Miss Gunn, I cannot think of a way to tell you this without causing distress, but seeing the ghost this evening is proof that you are turning wild."

Charlotte put the piece of paper on the blanket between them, drawing her legs up beneath her skirts so she could hug her knees. She took a deep breath, trying to soothe the panic that threatened to bubble up again. "But the Royal Society says there's no such thing as ghosts. I don't understand."

"As far as the masses are concerned, they don't exist. Only those that are turning wild see them. The Royal Society has pushed the idea that any ghostly activities can be explained by uncontrolled Latents, so that if someone reports seeing ghosts, they can be flagged up more easily for the Enforcers. It's illegal now, but before you and I were born, there used to be people who would earn a living from claims that they could communicate with the dead. No doubt many were charlatans, but the fact that they used to advertise such services tells you how much influence the Royal Society has now. The masses have been successfully convinced that ghosts are simply the province of fanciful storytelling and that anyone trying to profit from such is a criminal."

"Have you seen a ghost?"

He shook his head. "My ability was identified very early, Miss Gunn, and I was delivered to the Royal Society at a young age, long before there was any possibility of my turning. It's only those left unchecked who see them. It's why the Royal Society makes regular checks upon Bedlam and other such institutions. Poor souls considered to be going mad because they talk to people whom no one else can see may simply be manifesting atypically. They may not have set anything on fire, or destroyed anything by accident, but they are still Latents."

"Why didn't you tell me this before?"

He snorted. "Do you think it would have helped? It would have made you jump at every shadow." He looked away, gazing over the rolling hills. "And I confess I had hoped I could spare you the experience. I have been an arrogant fool, and I beg your forgiveness."

"There is nothing to forgive! You've been helping me."

When he looked back at her, the sadness in his eyes made her feel shaky and afraid again. "But I fear I misled you—not intentionally, you must understand that. But in my arrogance, I wanted to believe I could give you freedom from the Royal Society. I fear I cannot."

Charlotte gripped her legs tighter. "Are you abandoning your efforts? Is that what you're trying to say?"

"No!" He scrabbled onto his knees to face her, his earnest expression making him all the more beautiful. "I have no intention of doing that. But I cannot in good conscience allow you to believe that my efforts are guaranteed to be sufficient. No one else has ever done this, to my knowledge. I can teach you the techniques to stay calm and focused, but the Royal Society does more to Latents when they join, to stop them from turning wild, and I simply don't know what that is."

"How can you not know? Wasn't it done to you?"

His eyes were shadowed by his brow, darkening. "*Something* was done to me, Miss Gunn, but I do not understand it sufficiently to do the same to you."

The way he said it chilled her. "Is that what you are trying to protect me from?"

"In part." He looked up at the evening sky, sighing heavily. "I want to keep you from their clutches so that we can act independently. And safely. But if you've seen a ghost ... I don't know if that is even possible, let alone wise. As much as it pains me to say this, Miss Gunn, submitting to the Royal Society may be the only sensible option for you. For both of us."

"And what if I refuse?"

He closed his eyes, cutting off their light from her briefly, before he looked at her again. "I will help you as long as I can. But if you become a danger to yourself and others, I will have no choice but to report you myself."

She turned away from him, staring instead at the cornflowers bobbing near the hedgerow. First Ben, now Hopkins. Was there no hope for her? "I want to keep trying."

"Then you have my ardent support, Miss Gunn. But we will have to work harder and see each other more regularly. And that increases the risk."

She wondered if he was considering the same risks as she was. "I'm willing to take it, if you are."

"I am."

"But you must explain why you want to do this. There's something you're not telling me, Magus Hopkins. And given the conversation we find ourselves having now, I feel you should be open with me, so that I might fully understand all the risks involved."

He nodded. "That is entirely fair. I have kept you at arm's length, it's true. You have placed me in your confidence and I will do the same." He paused, shifting into a more comfortable position leaning to the side. His frock coat slid from his hip, revealing the top of his trousers and more of his waistcoat. Charlotte looked away, lest she stared too much. "I've suspected the Royal Society has been acting dishonourably for some time. I'm not willing to give details. Ignorance will protect you, should you be forced to submit. It isn't that I don't trust you. It's more that I wouldn't want to put you in an impossible position." He flicked a curl from his eyes and she could see he was finding it difficult. "I had a friend, in the Society, a fellow magus. She was . . . astonishing."

It felt like someone had punctured Charlotte's heart. He loved her. It was so obvious. Just thinking of her made his eyes shine. She swallowed down the lump in her throat. "Is she a Fine Kinetics magus, too?"

"She was," he said softly, and she realised with horror that she'd misunderstood. It wasn't their friendship that had ended. "One of the most talented I've ever met. You remind me of her, sometimes."

The slight twitch of a smile threatened to break her heart. Charlotte wanted to ask when and how, but even she wasn't so selfish. "What happened to her?"

"We became suspicious of certain . . . practices within the Society and we decided to investigate. The more we learned, the angrier she became. She wanted to blast through it like a storm, clear out the worst and force the Society to rebuild. I was the more cautious one. I held her back, constantly. In more ways than one. Then one day she lost her temper and threatened to expose someone very high up in the Society."

He stopped, leaving Charlotte hanging for his next words. "What happened?" she prompted.

"They killed her."

With him facing away from her, she couldn't see whether he was weeping, but his voice sounded strained.

"I'm so sorry," she whispered. "And they let you live?"

"Oh, they had no idea I was involved. We made sure of that. Neither one of us ever acted in a way that could incriminate the other. It was her care that saved me. And ever since I've been left with such knowledge that would be enough to make any man rage into the wind, and yet I am utterly powerless to do anything about it."

"Because they'd kill you?" She frowned at his nod. "But why would it be any different for me?"

"Because if we can keep you outside the Royal Society, Miss Gunn, they can't kill you the way they killed her."

"I don't understand."

He plucked another blade of grass. She wondered if he needed something else to focus upon, to make the conversation easier. "They do something to us, to stop us from turning wild. Whatever that is, it enables them to kill us. They don't even have to send someone to do it. They don't have to be in the same room or even the same city. One moment she was talking to me and the next . . ." He tossed the blade of grass away. ". . . she was dead."

"Are you sure it was them if—" His glare cut her off.

"I'm sorry, of course you're certain."

His regard softened. "I will do everything I can to keep you free of their power, Miss Gunn. But the one thing I will not do is stand by and do nothing if you fully turn wild. I've seen what it does and I could not bear to witness you suffering like that."

"I'll try harder," Charlotte said. "I'll fight it."

She wasn't sure if he was convinced, but he gave her an encouraging smile at least. "I know you will. And there's hope yet. This has only just happened. Unless this isn't the first time you've seen a ghost?"

A memory of the room the debtor's cage was in, the first time she saw it, returned to her. There had been a man standing in there who'd ignored her when she'd tapped on the window. Could he have been a ghost? "Would it make a difference if I've been seeing them for a long time?"

"I'd be more concerned. Have you?"

His worry was so touching. "No," she said, pushing the memory away. "But I will tell you if it happens again." She held the piece of paper out to him again. "Please may we talk about this, and what I'm to do? I can't bear the thought of Ben waiting for me. And that awful blackmailer will be expecting me at eleven bells, and I don't know what to do."

"Well," Hopkins said as he took the torn out page, "I think the easiest way to deal with that cad is to never go back there again. He doesn't know your real name and there's little chance of him seeing you again."

"But I have to help Ben."

Hopkins didn't respond, distracted by the symbols on the paper. "Good lord," he said, eyes widening. "These were on every machine?"

"All the ones I could check. I assume it's on all of them. What do they mean? Some of them reminded me of that cage mechanism."

Pressing his fist against his lips, Hopkins nodded. "Miss Gunn, did you find yourself more tired today after working the looms for the whole shift?" When she nodded, he waved the paper. "These symbols are the cause, not just the heat. As you worked the loom, a portion of your . . . spiritual energy, for want of a better phrase, was stolen by magic worked into the device."

"Stolen? I don't understand."

"These ones here, at the side, they were embossed into the drive belt, yes? They send that energy up to the line shaft. I'd wager there are sigils on the line shaft to carry it to the final destination. Imagine it's like tiny parts of your soul being actively pulled from you and sent up the line shaft in small, regular amounts." He tapped his fist against his lips. "It seems an honest day's labour is not enough for the Dynamics magi."

Charlotte thought of the other workers and how exhausted they were by the end of the day. It enraged her. "It's disgusting. No wonder everyone is so weak and unwell. But where is it being sent? What is it being used for?"

"I would imagine it's being stored—it must be, given the number of workers there. Some of it is probably used by the . . ." He trailed off, and Charlotte finished the sentence in her mind.

Used by the magi working the line shaft. Ben had looked so strong, so well, and she'd thought it was simply that he was finally happy and had a direction at last. Purpose. She shook her head. "Ben can't possibly know. He'd never support something as barbaric as this."

"I thought he looked very well," Hopkins said. "Did he explain his improvement in health?"

Charlotte didn't like Hopkins's tone. "He didn't need to. He simply got better. He's happy, that's all." She stood up. "You need to take me back to Manchester. He's waited long enough."

Hopkins stood, pocketing the paper so he could roll up the blanket. "We need to discuss our next steps."

"Well, I have to tell Ben. He needs to know what's happening there so he can put a stop to it."

"That's out of the question! How can you explain your knowledge to him? It would endanger both of us."

"But he needs to understand how awful the mill is before he fully commits to running it!"

"Miss Gunn, there's every chance that this is something done in all of Ledbetter's factories. How loyal to him is your brother?"

That gave her pause. "My brother is a good man," she said firmly. "I have every faith in him condemning this as strongly as we do."

She started off for the carriage, Hopkins falling into step alongside her. "Miss Gunn, I think you need to consider this more carefully. If you tell him, and he is loyal to Ledbetter, you're forcing him to choose whether to obey his master or respect his sister. Which do you think he is more likely to do?"

Doubting Ben was simply too much to bear. So she said nothing.

"Miss Gunn. Charlotte." His hand caught her arm and she stopped, her breath seized by his contact. "You need to face the possibility that he will side with Ledbetter, and if that happens, you will be in danger."

"Do you have such little faith in my brother?"

"Perhaps it's overwhelmed by a surfeit of care for you."

She blushed. Damn her ridiculous face! She was certain there was something she planned to say, but it escaped her. Fumbling for some words, her gaze fell upon the paper poking from his pocket. "Would you be willing to explain those symbols to me?"

"If you give me your word that you won't break into Ledbetter's estate and carve them into his furniture."

Was he joking or making a suggestion? The slow arching of his eyebrow made her laugh.

"Good lord, you actually considered it!" he said, and the blush deepened. "I'll show you in the carriage. But I beg you to not reveal your knowledge to your brother. Will you promise me that?"

She nodded. They climbed back inside and he was true to his word. It was all quite simple once he'd explained it, and her mind raced, fuelled by the new knowledge. "That cage . . . that's how it killed people, wasn't it? That mechanism sucked the life out of them all in one go, whereas the looms take a tiny amount each day."

"Yes, that's right."

"But how do you know this?"

He twisted the ring on his right hand. "It's something I've been investigating for some time."

She made the connection. "That's what you and your . . . friend were . . ." A brief nod was all she got, but it was enough. "That's why you hate Ledbetter so much."

"Oh, there are many reasons for that, my dear."

They shared a smile. She went back to studying the symbols. "If the looms take a tiny bit of someone's life, and that one there makes sure it can't be more than just a tiny bit, what would happen if someone died whilst they were working a loom?"

"An interesting question, Miss Gunn. Do you think

there's a connection between this and the ghosts in the factory?"

Nodding, she leaned back. The motion of the carriage, coupled with staring at the paper, had made her feel nauseous. "I saw a wisp above the loom when it was being destroyed. Is it too much of a leap to connect the two? Can ghosts move objects? Smash things?"

"I have no idea. But it's an interesting theory. Remind me of what that ghost lady said about the ones in the mill."

"She said they just kept screaming. And that they didn't listen to her. But she listened to me. I thought she was real, in fact. She didn't look like a ghost. She looked like a normal person. She just kept repeating herself. That was the only odd thing about her. And the fact that she died a few days ago, of course."

They shared another smile, this one tinged with a hint of guilt that they could find humour in something so morbid. "I find the difference interesting, if the ghost is to be believed."

"I heard them screaming. I believe her. I can't believe I'm having this conversation. I'm not going mad, am I?"

"Turning wild can drive you mad, not the other way round," Hopkins said. "Poor comfort, I know. The wisp you saw, above the loom, did it look like a person?"

"No. It looked like . . . steam from a kettle, but moving with purpose. What if the machines stole the part that keeps them . . . intact? Like the ghost I spoke to. She was intact. And she died in that bed." Charlotte shuddered at the thought of it. "Oh, I have to sleep in that bed tonight."

"You most certainly do not," Hopkins said firmly. "You will stay in a proper hotel. And if your brother does not arrange it, I will. Agreed?"

She nodded, already feeling guilty about the other ladies in her dorm who didn't have a handsome magus to look after them. "If the symbols were changed, so they took more than just a sliver, couldn't they absorb the wispy ghosts in the mill?"

"If your theory is correct, yes. Of course, you'd have to destroy the symbols afterwards, so they don't kill the person who works it the next day. And you'd have to work the loom and somehow trigger an incident."

Charlotte snapped her fingers. "I know how to do that! Pain. It's pain that triggers . . ." She thought it through. "Oh. I think I understand. The ghosts there may not be as intact as Betty was, but they're angry. They sounded tormented . . . I think they're attacking the looms because they don't want more people to be hurt and killed like they were. They're trying to protect their fellow workers." She clasped her hands together, disturbed.

"But they can't protect them," Hopkins said gently. "Only the living can do that. And these ghosts have killed more people by accident. It has to be stopped."

"Can you write down which symbols I'd need to change and how?"

He pulled a pencil from an inside pocket but didn't write anything straight away. "Miss Gunn, we need consider this very carefully. If you solve the problem at this mill, there won't be any pressure upon Ledbetter to improve them. There are people who are trying to achieve that. I spoke to one of them yesterday, in fact."

"Are you suggesting I don't do this?"

"I just—"

"Because I must. The people who work there are at risk, and if the incidents don't stop, that awful Paxton will use them to get my brother transported to Australia. I'm going to fix the problem, and then once Ben's position is secured, he can put a stop to this foul process."

Hopkins groaned. "He isn't going to change anything about the way the mills are run, because that is dictated by Ledbetter and he is the one behind all this! You saw the cage, you've seen these symbols! This is what he is, a thief, and one apprentice is not going to change anything."

Charlotte folded her arms. "We'll see about that. Please show me how to do it." When he hesitated again, she said, "Please, Magus Hopkins. I've made friends there and I feel bad enough about leaving them behind. I have to make sure that they are safe, as well as my brother, and this is the only way I can."

He started to draw. Charlotte could hear the city's thrum outside the carriage again. Ben would be beside himself by now.

Hopkins handed her the piece of paper. "Change this one to that and this one to that and it should do as you say. But remember, it will take any spiritual energy close to the loom, so you must run as quick as you can when you set it off. Once it's taken the excess energy, destroy the loom with your Dynamics, at a distance."

"What if I can't control myself afterwards?"

"I have every faith in you, Miss Gunn. Remember your marque. Here, draw it out whilst you can and look at it just before. I shall be in room twenty-five at the Grand Hotel all evening. If you run into any difficulties, get to me as soon as you can. Even if you fear you're turning. I will make sure you're safe. If all is well and your brother does the right thing and puts you in a hotel, send a message to me at the Grand. Say . . . 'The delivery of your cheeses will be made tomorrow.'"

"Cheeses?"

He shrugged. "It's the most harmless thing I can think of."

She folded the paper back up and tucked it into her dress. "Thank you, Magus Hopkins."

He took her hand and kissed it, his eyes flicking up to look at her as he did so. "Be careful, Miss Gunn."

Chapter 10

AS CHARLOTTE PICKED HER way back through the filth of the alleyway, she tried to think of a way to talk to Ben about the mill without incriminating Magus Hopkins. Remaining silent on the matter of the symbols on the looms was out of the question; she had to tell Ben what he was really getting into. But how could she broach it without getting anyone into trouble?

She had to explain to him what was causing the incidents, not only so he could protect himself against Paxton, but also to ensure that none of the innocent workers were going to be wrongfully prosecuted. She had the feeling Mags was a socialist, but Charlotte wasn't prepared to say anything about that. She agreed with Mags and there was no way she was going to endanger any efforts to improve working conditions.

By the time she got to the cottage it was almost dark. Charlotte knocked on the door, checking the street for any signs of someone following her. She couldn't see anyone. The door opened and she stepped inside. She didn't even have a chance to get to the front room before Ben had slammed the door shut. He embraced her fiercely.

"I've been beside myself with worry! Why are you so late?"

"Sorry. I had to rest after my shift, I was so tired," she lied. "And then when I did set out, someone from the mill followed me, so I had to put them off my trail. I got lost. I'm so sorry."

"Following you?" Ben went to the front room window and peeped out from the edge of the curtains. "Who?"

She had no idea who'd been following her before, but it was likely to be either Dotty, Mags, or the blackmailer. She didn't want to mention any of them. "I don't know. A man. I got away, though, and I'm certain he didn't follow me here."

Ben closed the curtains and moved the lantern to the centre of the room, setting it down between a new wooden chair and the armchair. "Well done. Oh, darling, you do look worn out. I feel terrible. Do you have any news?"

"I don't suppose you have any of those buns?"

He fetched a small bundle. After a bun and some more ginger beer, she felt better. She ate and drank quickly, pressured by his impatient fidgeting.

"I've heard that Paxton believes it's a Latent," he said, unable to wait any longer. "Do you agree?"

"No, it's not a Latent."

"You seem very certain."

There was suspicion in the way he looked at her, and it stung. "Ben, Paxton is an idiot who's desperate to pin this on someone who isn't powerful enough to fight back. He accused my friend, and it was only when another loom was destroyed that he realised it couldn't be her, because she was with him when it happened."

"And where were you?"

"In the mill. Ben, why are you looking at me like that?" Had the blackmailer mentioned something to him already? No, surely not.

"I don't know what you mean," Ben said.

"Like you don't trust me."

He sighed, leaning forwards with elbows on knees, resting his head on his hands. "I'm sorry. Ledbetter gave me a dressing down this afternoon. He's in the city and he wants answers."

She set down the bottle and came and knelt beside him, resting her hand on his back. He was under incredible pressure. "I'm trying to help, darling. Please don't take this out on me. I've been doing all I can and I'm not going to mislead you."

"I'm sorry, dear heart. I've been such a beast to you." He kissed her cheek. "Is there nothing you can tell me about what's causing these incidents? With two looms gone in as many days, Ledbetter's on the warpath. That damn Paxton knows just what to say to him, and I'm not like that. I'm not interested in one-upmanship and petty politics. I just want to work hard and better myself and look after my family. And look what I'm doing to you. You look ill, Charlie. What kind of a brother am I?"

She embraced him. "I understand, I really do. And I have made some progress." The hope in his eyes made her appreciate how desperate he was. She went back to the armchair. "It definitely isn't a socialist saboteur and it definitely isn't a Latent."

"Is it someone from Cartwright's?"

Charlotte shook her head as she stared at the dusty floorboards. If she told him her ghost theory, she'd have to admit having seen them. Given his comment yesterday about turning her in for testing, she didn't dare do that. "I don't know exactly," she said, making him groan. "But I can show you."

"I don't understand."

"I know what triggers the attacks. And I genuinely think it would best for you to see one; otherwise, it would be very hard for you to believe me."

He smoothed his moustache, thinking. "The mill is empty now. I could sneak you in. But another loom being destroyed will not go down well with Ledbetter."

"But isn't it worth the risk? I'm sure that if we both put our minds to it, we'll arrive at a solution. Better one loom now, than goodness knows how many before you're blamed. Perhaps if you saw one being destroyed, you'd be able to work out the cause better than I ever could." In reality, she hoped that if he saw it happen, any suspicion he still harboured about socialists would be wiped away. Perhaps, if she did it carefully enough, she'd be able to steer him towards the same conclusion she'd reached. It was always the best way to convince Father or George about anything: she would simply present certain details and let them think they'd come to the clever solution. She wasn't sure that would ever work with Hopkins, though.

"Very well," Ben said, rising from his seat. "If you really do think I need to see this, we should go now. Ledbetter is at a function and Paxton is at the club. Let's go out the back, just in case anyone did follow you."

After taking her to the back of the cottage and extinguishing the lantern, Ben led her through a stinking communal backyard and out onto the street. It was dark now, making it easier for them to walk without fear of being spotted. He buttoned his overcoat to cover his striped cravat and she covered her head with her shawl, hiding as much of her face as she could. She had to hurry to keep up with his long strides, and her legs soon ached again, but soon they were at the fancy entrance to the mill.

Ben unlocked the door and ushered her inside to lock

it again behind them. It was dark, with only a tiny amount of light reaching the interior from the street's gas lamps. Knowing the space well, Ben guided her through the entrance hall and down a corridor in which he relit the lantern. She recognised the door they'd stopped in front of; it was the one that she'd seen from the other side in the mill itself. He unlocked it and she followed him inside.

It was silent in the mill, much to Charlotte's relief, and very dark. She was glad that Ben was with her. He shielded the side of the lantern that faced the windows on the far side. The shadows it cast made his face look unfamiliar and Charlotte shuddered.

"Show me, then, Charlie," he whispered.

She would have preferred to go to a loom that people thought was cursed, but the only one she was aware of had been destroyed earlier that day. The one nearest to them was as good as any, so she went over to it. "This may sound very strange," she said in a whisper. "But I believe that pain triggers an incident. When I was beaten by the foreman, he knocked me into the loom and then the . . . strangeness started."

Ben's sigh conveyed how unimpressed he was. "Oh, Charlie, did you really bring me here to listen to such a fanciful story? It was just a coincidence."

"Stand back," she said. "And I'll prove it to you."

He did as she asked, and Charlotte went to the loom at the end of the row. After steeling herself, she raised her arm and hit it against the cast-iron frame as hard as she could bear to. She winced, knowing that another impressive bruise would bloom there tomorrow, and waited.

She heard the screaming first, and there was a change in the quality of the lantern light, as if mist were rising inside the mill. A glance at Ben told her that he heard nothing, so she masked her fear, trying her best to ignore how the sound built in volume until the loom shuddered. She jumped back from it and then Ben pulled her to him, wrapping an arm around her protectively as the loom creaked and the threads snapped.

Above it, the mist was coalescing and changing shape constantly. Wispy tendrils peeled off and shot towards the loom and the wood splintered at the points of contact. She felt Ben jolt with each impact, his grip around her tightening. All the while, the screeching was growing louder and she wanted to cover her ears, but she forced herself not to, lest Ben wonder why. Once the wooden frames were broken, hanging useless in a tangle of cotton threads from the iron frame, the violence stopped. The haze above the machine dissipated but not the noise. Charlotte struggled to ignore the continuing screams as Ben let her go and went over to the loom.

"Good God in heaven," he whispered, staring at it.

"That's the first time I've actually witnessed it."

Charlotte leaned against the wall, relieved that the sound of the ghosts had faded as she listened to Ben. She recalled the first incident she'd witnessed, and how there had been only one wisp. She wondered if she simply hadn't noticed the rest, or whether it was because the machines were in motion. If that was a factor, why hadn't the ghost been sucked in? Then she recalled that the drive belt had snapped, thus breaking the connection to the line shaft.

"Charlie? Shall we find you a chair?"

Dear, sweet Ben had mistaken her thoughtful silence for shock. "Do you know what could cause that?" she asked.

He shook his head. "I have no idea. You were right about the pain . . . how utterly bizarre. You're not badly hurt, are you?"

"No." She went over to look at the loom with him. How could she explain what had happened without jeopardising herself? He was holding the lantern close to the loom, inspecting the damage. "Ben, something about these looms is . . . odd." She pointed to the symbols on the drive belt. "Have you noticed these marks before?"

"They're from the manufacturing process," he said with barely a glance.

"They do something to the workers," she said and he

diverted his attention fully to her. "Darling . . . you need to know about this. I think these looms steal the life from people, literally, just a tiny amount each day. I know that sounds ridiculous, but that's why everyone is so exhausted and why they are ill."

"Whatever gives you that idea?"

She paused. He didn't laugh or even look like he disbelieved her. Perhaps he thought she was being overdramatic. "Do you believe me?" He didn't immediately respond, but she knew him too well for the silence to hide anything. She covered her mouth. "Oh, Ben," she whispered through her fingers. "You knew, didn't you?"

"It is far more complicated than you understand, Charlotte," he said, his back straightening as if he could shrug off the shame with good posture.

"That's why you're so strong now, isn't it? Is this what you meant by your breakthrough? How could you steal life from these poor people? They're treated badly enough without this! It's despicable!"

"How dare you judge me when you know nothing of the challenges we face!"

"What challenges? Making the most money?"

"I meant we as in magi, Charlotte. And I include you in that. This is a humane solution to—"

"Humane? I beg to differ!"

"You have no right to judge me when you won't take

responsibility for what you are and the damage you can do!"

"It's under control!"

He leaned closer, lowering his voice lest they both start shouting. "More than during my test? Or the month before that? Don't you remember how many people died in our street?"

"There was a flu epidemic. What does that have to do with—"

"Don't you remember our neighbour dying on the very same day of my testing? You obviously haven't noticed the pattern. You killed them, Charlie. This is what happens if you try to do too much."

She moved away from him, feeling nauseous. "I don't believe you."

"When I came home, half dead, only your nursing had any effect. Now I understand that I took spiritual energy from you, and to save yourself, you took from everyone around us. It's exactly the same as this place, only here it's controlled; only a tiny amount is taken from each person each day. This way, the mill can function without killing any elderly people in the vicinity."

Charlotte could only shake her head, speechless. Ben sighed and cautiously rested a hand on her shoulder. "You need to report yourself, Charlie."

"No one else has died, or even been ill!"

"That's because you don't have to keep me alive anymore. What about when you finally lose control?"

Hopkins hadn't mentioned any of this. Ben was trying to distract her. "Stop making this about me. We have a problem to solve here and now. Is there any way these symbols could be the cause?"

Reluctantly, he directed his attention back towards the loom. "I don't see how."

She suppressed a frustrated groan. "People have died, whilst working the looms, haven't they? Before any of these incidents started?" When he nodded, she pointed at the symbols. "What if when they die, a sliver of their soul is taken but the rest is left behind?"

"Not soul, Charlie. Spiritual energy." Scratching his chin, Ben looked at the symbols. "That could be why pain triggers this, I suppose. Perhaps something of those people is left behind and doesn't want anyone else to suffer the same fate. It seems . . . bizarre, but I cannot think of any other explanation."

"The workers think some of the looms are cursed, and the attacks do seem to cluster. As George always says, clustering gives us clues. Perhaps if someone died at a loom and something was left behind, then maybe they watch those ones more closely and react violently when someone gets hurt. That makes the pattern."

"Yes, it makes sense." He looked at her. "How did you

know about the symbols, Charlie?"

"It's a very long story and one that I don't want to share here. Let's focus on this problem."

He nodded, but she could tell he wasn't happy about it. "I know what the symbols do, but I'm not very good at altering them. I find that part of my training quite difficult. I suppose I should tell Ledbetter about this theory, and then he can decide what to do."

"No, that's not enough. You need to prove you're more capable than Paxton. I have an idea about how to stop this from happening again." She paused, hating the tension between them. "If I do this for you, will you promise you won't report me to the Royal Society?"

He looked horrified. "I cannot promise that! It would be irresponsible."

"Can't you trust me to do the right thing if the time comes?"

"I fear you won't realise when that is." He looked down into her eyes. "Oh, Charlie Bean. You're putting me in such a difficult position. I love you. I want you to be safe and happy and fulfilled. You could have all of that in the Royal Society."

"I would rather find my safety and fulfilment with George. Please, Ben. I've done so much for you. Can't you do this for me?" Pressing his lips tight together, he nodded. She breathed more easily. "You need to leave the lantern with me and stand right back."

"What are you planning to do?"

"I'm going to make some alterations. Once the loom is going again, you need to keep back until it stops. Otherwise, it could kill you. Go on, stand back. Let me do this without worrying about you."

Reluctantly, Ben gave her the lantern and retreated into the shadows along the back wall whilst she moved to the next loom along. She recalled the two new symbols that Hopkins had drawn for her as she took one of the shuttles, opened it and pulled off the bobbin. She broke off the metal spike and held it like a pencil as she searched for the first of the symbols to alter. It was on a cog at the side of the loom and scratching the amendment took a little effort, but it was manageable.

She found the second symbol on the drive belt and was aware of Ben watching as she altered it. They were going to have a very difficult conversation about this, but that was something to worry about another time. Tucking the spike into her waistband, Charlotte held up the lantern and checked her work.

The machine needed to be started, but she feared using her ability would make her more prone to turning wild. "Can you start this by moving the drive belt?" she asked Ben. "You must stand back, though. Don't come close to the machine—it will be dangerous."

"What about you?"

"I'll trigger an attack and then run. I'll be fine."

The drive belt started to turn, making the loom spring into life. Charlotte hit her other arm against the frame as before and then dashed up the row as the screeching started again. When she was more than halfway down the row, she turned to watch the wisps gathering above the loom.

Someone grabbed her hair, exploiting the distraction to sneak up behind her. "I knew ye were up to sommat!" Horcombe said in her ear.

He must have been lurking outside, looking for her as he waited for his sovereign. She reached back to try to pull her hair free of his hands, but he merely grabbed one of her wrists and twisted her arm behind her back sharply, making her cry out. "This isn't what you think it is!" She gasped.

"You can explain it all to Magus Ledbetter 'imself. Apprentice Paxton is fetchin' 'im now. You're done for, ye Cartwright bitch!"

Charlotte remembered the large metal pin tucked into her waistband and plucked it out with her free hand, jabbing it behind her. With a yell, he threw her forwards to crash into one of the looms, winding her. All she could do was grab the iron frame as the pain filled her chest. Fearing that Ben would run past the doctored loom to get to her attacker, Charlotte looked for him in the shadows, but he was out of sight. She struggled to draw a breath as Horcombe approached.

In the background, she was aware of the screeching fading and risked a glance at the loom to see the cloud of wisps being sucked into the frame with each attempted strike. It was working!

A blow came out of nowhere, knocking her down onto her bruised hip, and she couldn't help but cry out in pain again. Horcombe was standing near her feet, poised to strike her again, when Ben appeared behind him and pinned his arms. With relief, Charlotte realised that her brother had kept his head, and instead of just careering up the row of looms like a mad bear, he'd crept down the next row along to take Horcombe by surprise.

Ben was strong, but it was clear that Horcombe had done some brawling in his time. He didn't stay pinned for long, knocking his head back to crunch his skull against Ben's nose, making her brother roar in pain and let go.

"Blood and sand!" Horcombe said at the sight of him. "And you an apprentice! I don't know what Cartwright is payin' yer, but I bet it won't be worth the lashin' you'll get from Ledbetter!"

"You imbecile," Ben said, blood pouring out of his nose. "You have no idea what's happening here."

"Oh, don't I?" Horcombe stood, fists up, light on his

feet like a boxer. "It all makes sense now. I couldn't work out 'ow a Latent could get a job 'ere, but I suppose y'brought 'er in to help yer."

"What are you talking about?"

"Don't pretend you don't know." Horcombe sneered. "Y'think I'm stupid. I saw what she did to that loom this mornin'!"

Charlotte pulled herself up by clutching the iron frame, finally able to draw a breath. The screeching of the ghosts was fading rapidly, and as Ben squared off against Horcombe, she risked another look at the loom. There was only the faintest haze above it now, and the loom itself was undamaged. The new symbols had sucked the wisps into the line shaft before they could do any damage.

"I can't wait to tell Apprentice Paxton that you were in on this," Horcombe said. "He'll be 'ere any moment, and you'll be clapped in irons before the night is out, you and that Latent bitch." He laughed. "Yeah, I can see how scared you are. Go on! Tell me I'm wrong. Tell me I'm stupid. Go on!"

Ben was staring at Horcombe with the most terrifying, murderous glare. "I don't think you're stupid," he said. "I think you are dangerous."

With a contemptuous flick of a wrist, Ben sent one of the metal buckets full of empty bobbins flying into Horcombe's face. It knocked him down, and Ben sent another whistling past Charlotte, who leaned back in shock. It hit Horcombe's side and then pushed him down the row away from her, bringing him to a stop next to the working loom.

"No!" Charlotte cried out as she watched the colour drain from Horcombe's startled face. She focused on the loom's drive belt and snapped it as quick as she could, but by the time the machine rattled to a stop, she could see he wasn't breathing.

Charlotte ran over to kneel beside him and held her hand over his mouth. There was no breath. She looked up at Ben, distraught, who approached slowly.

"Is he dead, Charlie?"

She nodded, tears running down her cheeks as he leaned against the loom opposite. "What are we going to do?"

He stared down at the body. His nose was bleeding from the blow and he was very pale, but he didn't seem at all upset. "Did it work, do you think? Your plan, I mean?"

"Ben, you just killed a man!" she whispered.

"But did it work?"

Was he in shock? Yes, that had to be it. "I think so. It sucked the life from him, so it must have sucked in the excess spirits, too." She stopped at the sound of a door opening on the other side of the mill.

"Paxton and Ledbetter!" Ben hissed. "Run, hide, before they see you! I'll take care of this."

Aching, Charlotte scrambled to her feet. She had just enough time to dive into the shadows against the far wall, before Ledbetter and Paxton arrived at the other end of the row.

"Gunn?" Ledbetter called. "What's to do?" He was wearing white tie, which somehow didn't suit him, and had a pale cream folder tucked under his arm.

"I've solved the mystery, Master Magus Ledbetter," Ben said, bowing as the huge man headed towards him with Paxton in tow. "It was a Latent."

"A girl, that's what I was told," Paxton said.

"Who's that?" Ledbetter pointed at the body.

"He's the one who came and told me somethin' was goin' on," Paxton said, throwing a suspicious look at Ben.

"He lured a mill girl in here and threatened her," Ben said. "I heard a commotion and came to investigate. He was smashing that loom. The poor girl was scared out of her wits. He was telling her he'd smash her skull against the wall if she didn't say she was a saboteur working for Cartwright. I challenged him, there was a scuffle and he tried to kill me. I . . . fear I overreacted, Master Magus Ledbetter. I threw those buckets at him with my ability, and it killed him. I accept full responsibility."

From her hiding place, Charlotte could see the triumphant gloating on Paxton's face as Ledbetter approached the body.

The mage nudged the body with his shoe. "Old, for a Latent. Not unheard of, though. Paxton, go to the police station on Fairfield Street and ask for Chief Constable Jenkins to come right away. Tell 'im it's me that wants 'im. Don't tell 'im why. Just say it's important."

Paxton did not look pleased about this. "Should I not say there's been a murder so that—"

Ledbetter cuffed him round the head. "No, you should bloody not! Do as I say, Paxton, else I'll have another body to explain to Jenkins, d'you 'ear?"

"Yes, Master Magus Ledbetter," Paxton mumbled resentfully and turned to go.

"Get a move on!" Ledbetter bellowed, and Paxton broke into a run.

Ledbetter moved back to look at Horcombe, then Ben. "Right, then, m'boy. Why don't you tell me what really 'appened before the Peeler gets 'ere?"

The lantern light picked out the sheen of sweat on Ben's forehead. "He isn't a Latent," he said. "He thought the mill girl was one, and had been watching her. She was a witness to one of the incidents." He pointed at the body. "That man assumed she was coming in here to sabotage the looms and ran off to get you without my knowledge. In fact, I had asked her to meet me here and describe exactly what she saw, without the foreman breathing down her neck."

Ben paused, and Charlotte bit her lip. *Please don't tell him the truth*, she silently begged him.

"Go on, son," Ledbetter said. "Paxton's not 'ere, you can be straight wi'me."

"The girl described what she saw and I dismissed her. There was no way she was a Latent, and besides, I was already forming a theory about what was happening here. Talking to her made it all come together in my mind. I tested my theory." He pointed at the broken loom. "I'm very sorry about the damage, Master Magus, I'll reimburse you from my stipend. You see, the incidents haven't been caused by saboteurs or a hidden Latent. The problem is esoteric in nature. It's all to do with spiritual energy system, sir. It's geared to take only a tiny part each day, but we haven't considered what happens at the point of death. From the girl's testimony, I discovered that pain in the vicinity of the loom is the trigger. My theory is that when a worker dies, some of their spiritual energy is absorbed into the system, but because of the gating mechanism, only a tiny part can be taken and the rest is left here. En masse, these remnants attack the machines. The attacks have been worsening as more workers have died, steadily worsening the problem."

Charlotte's face was hot with anger. Not only did Ben

know about what the symbols on the looms did, he sounded like an expert! And now that he was explaining the cause of the problems, Ledbetter would be unstoppable!

But she couldn't blame Ben for telling the truth; what else could he say? Besides, he needed to impress Ledbetter to save his own neck. She was more annoyed with herself. How would she explain this to Hopkins? It was exactly what he didn't want to happen!

"I altered the gating mechanism on that loom," Ben continued, pointing at the one next to the body, "and set it off, after striking my arm against it, just as I had with the previous one. I watched from a distance, and as you can see, no damage was done. The excess spiritual energy has been taken into the system. That loom hasn't been reset, by the way."

Ledbetter went over to the altered loom, inspecting it. "Go on," he prompted.

"Well, this man came back in the middle of my test and assumed that I was in fact behind it all. He accused me of being one of Cartwright's people. He was one of Paxton's stooges, it seems, and delighted in telling me how Paxton would see to it that I was destroyed. I told the truth before, sir. He struck me, and whilst there was an element of self-defence, I was simply furious with him for saying such things. I used the buckets to knock him away, forgetting the loom alteration, and he landed here. His spiritual energy was sucked into the system before I could do anything. I feel absolutely dreadful."

Charlotte watched Ledbetter as Ben confessed. He moved with the lantern, examining the cogs at the side and then inspecting the broken drive belt, his attention lingering over her alterations. He nodded to himself as her stomach cramped. She knew nothing about those symbols and could only pray that the ones Hopkins had given her were generic, not specialised to him.

Ben wiped his forehead with a handkerchief and then dabbed at the blood under his nose, wincing. Ledbetter set down the lantern next to the folder he'd brought in with him and went over to him.

"You didn't say this in front of Paxton. Why?"

"Well, sir, if I may be so bold, I hoped that my solution would earn me my qualification, leaving him out in the cold. If I told you there was a problem of an esoteric nature, one that all your mills are vulnerable to, he could take that information elsewhere and profit from it at your expense. I decided to wait and tell you the truth when we were alone."

Ledbetter grinned, the shadows cast by the lantern making him ghoulish. "Benjamin Gunn, you 'ave done sterlin' work here, m'boy. Don't you worry about a thing. I've got an understandin' with the constable, nowt will come of it." When Ben didn't look relieved, Ledbetter rested a hand on his shoulder. "He's just a mill worker, son. No one'll care. We'll get this sorted. In the mornin' you're to come wi'me to the college to write up all y'said 'ere. I'll see to it that they give you full qualification and a bonus to your stipend. I'll personally fund your first mill. You've done me a great service, m'boy, a great service and I'll see to it that you'll want for nothin.'"

Ben blinked at him as Ledbetter took his hand and pumped it up and down, clapping him on the arm. "Thank you, Master Magus Ledbetter," he stammered.

"I knew you'd come good. Knew you'd be sommat special, right from the day I tested yer. You've a bright future, young man. I can see the upper echelons of the college for you, one day. Just keep workin' 'ard and thinkin' sharp under pressure, and you'll go far. Paxton ent good for anythin' save workin' the shafts. I'll make sure he's tucked away where his jealousy can't touch you. A'right?"

Ben nodded, managing a smile now. "Thank you, sir. Thank you very much."

The sound of the door opening at the other end of the mill made Ledbetter step away. "That'll be the Peeler. Let me do the talkin' and leave some of that blood under y'nose so he can see it. C'mon."

He started to steer Ben away, but then hurried back

to pick up the folder, looking worried. After a moment's deliberation, Ledbetter tucked it under one of the pristine looms across the way. He obviously didn't want to be seen with it. What was in there?

Ben glanced back, and she could see his eyes scan the darkness, looking for her whilst Ledbetter was distracted. He surreptitiously pointed towards the door they'd come through before, signalling to her that she should leave that way, seeing as the policemen and Paxton were over at the worker's entrance. No doubt Paxton had wanted to make sure that no one saw a Peeler enter through the posh doors.

Charlotte waited until he and Ledbetter were on their way before scurrying over to the place the folder was hidden. There was a sheaf of papers inside that looked formal, with the College of Dynamics coat of arms stamped at the top. Hearing the conversation come to an end at the far side of the mill and footsteps begin, she only dared look at the top page. The title *Project 84* was in a large font with *Progress report: Carnforth Hall* typed in smaller text below. A TOP SECRET stamp in red ink was on the top right corner of the page. She closed the folder and tucked it back into its hiding place exactly as she'd found it before dashing off to the door. The group of men were at the top of the row as she reached it, but remembering the well-oiled hinges from when they came in before, Charlotte took the risk and opened it to slip out of the mill unseen.

She ran back to the cottage, thinking that Ben would come looking for her there as soon as he could get away. It wasn't until she sat on the back step and caught her breath that the image of the man's dead face returned to her. Huddled against the door in the darkness, Charlotte wept until exhaustion finally claimed her and she fell asleep.

Chapter 11

CHARLOTTE STARED AT THE sumptuous breakfast laid out on the crisp white linen. From the third-floor window of the hotel, she could look out over St Peter's Field, the red-bricked mills over on the far side a mere backdrop to the peaceful scenery. She wondered if Ben had chosen this room in particular in an effort to put the mill far from her mind.

It wasn't working.

She was hungry but strangely without appetite. She picked at the poached eggs, thinking of Mags and Dotty who would have already been at work for hours. They'd be wondering where she was. Mags had probably told them all of what she'd said about Betty. Maybe they all thought she was too scared of the ghost to go back. It was a decent enough explanation, given the circumstances.

Last night she had been so grateful that she didn't have to go back to the lodging house. Ben had found her on the cottage back step and brought her to the hotel right away, even running the bath for her. Once she was clean and tucked up in the cloud-soft bed, they'd finally talked.

It had felt like a strange reversal to have him sitting there, hale and hearty, as she'd felt half dead.

"Everything is going to be fine," he'd said to her. "No charges will be pressed and I should be fully qualified by tomorrow evening."

She'd kept her opinions on the corruption of the police to herself. She didn't want him to get into trouble, but she didn't like the way that Ledbetter could brush a death aside like that.

"You heard the conversation between us?" he'd asked.

"Yes. I suppose you want me to tell you about the changes I made to the symbols, for your report."

"Please, Charlie. If you write them down for me, I'll handle everything else."

What else could she do? She wasn't going to send him back to Ledbetter empty-handed. He'd fetched some of the hotel letter paper from the desk, torn off the design at the top so it was blank and handed it to her with a pencil.

Poised to draw them, she'd stopped and looked at him. "Ben . . . I'll write these down but you have to understand . . . I can't tell you how I know about this."

He'd pursed his lips in disapproval. "No one outside of the Royal Society should know anything about them."

"Things aren't always the way they should be, are they? I'm certain that apprentices aren't supposed to put their sisters to work in a mill to solve their problems, either."

"I'll turn a blind eye if you'll forgive me," he'd finally said with a sigh.

"Then I'll write them down for you. But don't forget your promise. I will be happy with George and I won't ever use my abilities. Especially now I know the risks."

They'd embraced, and it had felt like she was holding her brother again.

Now, pushing cold poached eggs around her plate, Charlotte worried about whether she'd done the right thing, whilst simultaneously failing to think of an alternative. Perhaps the only thing to do was just accept that Ledbetter was going to benefit from her efforts, but more important, that her brother's safety was assured. She ignored the little voice at the back of her mind grumbling about how her brother always seemed to benefit more than she did. Silly voice. It knew nothing about the way things worked.

Tackling some toast, Charlotte focused on more positive things. As soon as she was home, she'd start writing up her experiences in the mill and sketch scenes from the memories that plagued her now. She'd make a chapbook and see if her agent could do something with it. It was a place to start. At the very least, if it was published, she'd send the proceeds to Dotty and Mags in the hope it would help them find a way out of that life. She had every intention to visit Ben's mill once it was running to see if things were better there. If they weren't, he'd have hell to pay. Still, she feared it would not be enough.

Ben couldn't escort her to the train station, having such an important day ahead of him, but he'd made all the arrangements for her to get there and to be picked up at Euston. It was a relief to climb into her first-class compartment, the trials of the trip behind her. She was bruised and still so very tired, barely able to keep her eyes open. She just wanted to go home and sleep in her own bed.

The sound of the compartment door opening woke her, and a smartly dressed middle-aged lady was helped into the compartment by a young man. They exchanged polite smiles and Charlotte watched as the lady waved him off.

"My son," she said. "He's a good boy."

The whistle blew, just at the moment Charlotte remembered that she was supposed to send a message to Hopkins at the Grand to assure him of her well-being. She silently cursed herself, but it was too late now. When they stopped at Crewe she'd send a telegraph to him.

The door opened a second time and a bag landed in the middle of the compartment, tossed inside from a hurrying passenger. In a swirl of burgundy and black satin, Hopkins clambered in and shut the door quick, receiving a glare from the station guard for his trouble.

"I do beg your pardon," he said to the other lady, whose stern expression was enough to make Charlotte shrink further back into her seat out of sympathy for Hopkins. "May I share this compartment with you and your sister?"

The lady began to reappraise Hopkins. "This young lady is not my sister, sir. We happen to be sharing this compartment." She looked at Charlotte. "Do you have any objection, dear?"

"Not at all," Charlotte replied. "Are you both travelling as far as London?"

"I shall be alighting at Crewe," the lady said and looked pointedly at Hopkins.

"Oh, I shall be travelling further than that," he said. "But if it pleases you, miss, I shall move to another compartment when our companion leaves."

The lady looked at him with obvious approval now. "Mrs Harper-Symthe," she said, extending a gloved hand to Hopkins, who kissed it dutifully.

"Magus Hopkins, of the Royal Society of Esoteric Arts," he said and the lady smiled in delight.

"A magus! How thrilling!"

He stifled a yawn, somehow managing to look devastatingly handsome as he did so. "My apologies, Mrs Harper-Symthe. I had a terrible night's sleep, worrying about a cheese delivery."

Charlotte blushed, knowing that had been directed at her, but neither of them looked at her.

"Tell me," Hopkins said to the lady. "Do you reside in Manchester?"

They talked without pause from Manchester to Crewe and Charlotte watched in fascinated silence as Hopkins worked a different sort of magic. By the time he helped Mrs Harper-Smythe out at Crewe, she was clearly infatuated with him and looked like she might abandon her plans, just to stay a moment longer with him. He helped her to find a porter and kissed her hand again, making the poor lady titter like a bird. When Hopkins got back into the compartment, he looked as if he'd spent the better part of the last hour in quiet contemplation, rather than waging a charm offensive.

"My apologies, Miss Gunn," he said once he was settled into his seat. "I barely had the opportunity to think, let alone draw you into the conversation."

"Indeed, you were far too busy ensuring that Mrs Harper-Smythe fell in love with you."

He fought a smile as the guard's whistle blew. Once the train was leaving the station, he relaxed. "I accept your apology for failing to reassure me of your well-being."

She blushed again. "I am sorry. I didn't have the opportunity last night and I confess it slipped my mind this morning. I do feel terrible about it."

With a little wave, he dismissed the topic. "Tell me everything."

And she did, ending it with another apology. "Now Ledbetter's mills will be the most successful in the country and it's my fault."

"But your brother is safe, and whilst the workers won't see much improvement in conditions, they won't be terrorised by anything supernatural at least."

"You're not angry?"

He shuffled along the seats until he was sat opposite her. "Miss Gunn, you have acted with honour and bravery. Yes, a man died, but he was blackmailing you."

"Hardly a capital offence!"

"Yes, but he would be alive now if he'd kept to himself. And in my humble opinion, your safety and well-being are far more important."

She didn't know what to say, so she fiddled with the lace on her cuff.

"Besides," Hopkins said, leaning back to look out of the window instead, "the mills are not the only pie that Ledbetter has his finger in. I've come across something I'd like to look into with you, if you're amenable?" When she gave an enthusiastic nod, he leaned forwards again, an excited twinkle in his eye. "I don't know exactly what it is yet, but I have a feeling that the syphoning off of spiritual energy has something to do with a 'Project 84.'"

Charlotte jolted. "I forgot about that! He had a file with him and I managed to peep inside while he talked to the policeman. It had 'Project 84' written on it and then . . . oh, what was it? And 'Progress report: Carnforth Hall' written underneath."

Hopkins looked at her as if she had just presented him with a diamond. "Miss Gunn, you never cease to surprise me! Excellent work! I shall look into that right away!" He took both of her hands and kissed them. "Well done," he said, giving them a gentle squeeze before letting go.

Charlotte was glad to be back in her heavy petticoats and crinoline. Without them, she feared she would have floated up to the ceiling and been forced to stay there for the remainder of the journey. As it was, duly weighted down, she and Hopkins spent a good portion of the trip back to London picking apart the events in the mill, her brother's prospects and what could be done to stop her from turning wild. She almost asked him about whether it was true that she could have been responsible for the deaths of their neighbours, but she couldn't bring herself to do it. Charlotte didn't want to think about it, nor mention anything that might take the light from his eyes as he spoke to her.

At the last stop before Euston, he kissed her hand one last time. "I should sit in a different compartment, Miss Gunn. As much as enjoy your company, I think it would be unwise for your father to see us travelling together. But I will see you in Covent Garden the day after tomorrow, yes?"

"Yes, of course," she'd said, and kept a smile on her face until she was alone again. She slumped in the corner, suddenly bereft. It was the longest she'd ever spent in his company and he'd laughed and smiled far more than ever before. It must be the relief, she thought. It couldn't possibly be anything else.

As the train pulled into Euston, Charlotte retied the bow on her bonnet and smoothed her dress. She pinched her cheeks, not wanting her father to see how pale she was, and opened the door's window as the train came to a stop.

"Charlotte!"

But that wasn't her father! George's voice came to her through the crowd and she waved happily when she caught sight of him. He looked so happy to see her! He came to the door and opened it for her, helping her out to embrace her. She winced at the contact with her bruises, but hid it well enough. "George, darling! What a lovely surprise! I've missed you so!"

"Charlotte, I have the most wonderful news," he said, holding her at arm's length so he could see her face. "I've been promoted! I am now officially a fully qualified registrar. We can marry!"

Mirroring her delighted smile, he embraced her again, this time lifting her into the air in his joy. Over his shoulder, she saw Magus Hopkins alight from the train. He gave her the briefest smile and looked away, plunging into the crowd and out of sight.

It felt like he was pulling something with him, right out of her chest. For one fanciful moment, she even considered running after him, but to what end? What was she thinking?

George set her down and she reached up to cup his face in her hands, reminding herself of what she had and what she was fighting so hard to keep. She saw the happiness and kindness in his eyes, felt his steady strength radiating from him. "I am so proud of you, my darling," she said. "And I am so happy. Let's go tell Mother and Father. We shall raise a glass to celebrate."

"We can discuss the wedding with them," George said, pulling her bag from the compartment.

"I could want nothing more," she answered, forcing herself to focus on him, so her traitorous eyes stopped scanning the crowd for a last glimpse of burgundy. "Nothing more at all."

About the Author

Photograph by Lou Abercrombie

EMMA NEWMAN writes dark short stories and science fiction and urban fantasy novels. She won the British Fantasy Society Best Short Story Award 2015, and *Between Two Thorns,* the first book in Emma's Split Worlds urban fantasy series, was shortlisted for the British Fantasy Best Novel and Best Newcomer 2014 awards. Her first science fiction novel, *Planetfall,* was published by Roc in 2015, and her second, *After Atlas,* was short-listed for the 2017 Arthur C Clarke Award. Emma is an audiobook narrator and also cowrites and hosts the Hugo-nominated, Alfie Award–winning podcast *Tea and Jeopardy,* which involves tea, cake, mild peril and singing chickens. Her hobbies include dressmaking and playing RPGs. She blogs at www.enewman.co.uk and can be found as @emapoca-lyptic on Twitter.

TOR · COM

Science fiction. Fantasy. The universe.

And related subjects.

*

More than just a publisher's website, *Tor.com* is a venue for **original fiction, comics,** and **discussion** of the entire field of SF and fantasy, in all media and from all sources. Visit our site today—and join the conversation yourself.